MW00967442

P.R.Morehouse

You may know or have heard of someone who has recently died in a car accident - their sudden death may very well have been a Triple Indemnity murder for profit, business decision by the syndicate.

The Triple Indemnity Murders

DELTA
Publishing

First Original Edition

Copyright© 2017 by Philip R. Morehouse

All rights reserved. This book may not be reproduced in any form, in whole or in part (beyond that copying permitted by U.S. Copyright Law, Section 107, "fair use" in teaching or research. Section 108, certain library copying, or in published media by reviewers in limited excerpt) without written permission from the author and/or publisher or estate of the author.

This is a work of fiction. Any resemblance to any actual place or person living or dead is strictly coincidental.

ISBN-13: 978-1981487424

ISBN-10: 1981487425

Published by Delta Press LLC

The Triple Indemnity Murders

Table of Contents

Disclaimer:
This is a work of fiction. Any caricature or resemblance to any actual person living or dead is strictly coincidental. Any reference to an incident or happening within a named city, village, place or thing(s) within this story, is purely fictional.

Dedication
This novel is dedicated to my mother who raised all four of us to do unto others as you would have them do unto you. She was a women dedicated to helping others; putting them first before herself.

Dear Friends
Thank you, for enduring my long absences while writing this book and for encouraging me in this pursuit.

A Very Special Thanks:
To my editor, Norma Cushner, who lets nothing get by her, and whose efforts have led to the enhanced readability of this story.

In addition, a special thanks to Lori Snowden, my cover designer, whose work serves as the billboard that attracts my readers to the story within.

The author, having once been a licensed insurance broker, has drawn on his vast experience of insurance law, types of policies and the day to day life of a Debit Collections insurance man in writing this unique, one of a kind story.

Chapter 1.0

T his was not going to be a business as usual day, only Ryker Massey didn't know it yet, but his life was about to change in a way that not even he could not have imagined.

Today was Thursday - it was the day that all "new" business sales were reported and Ryker had no new business to report. In the eyes of his Sales Manager, Pete Fordson and the District Manager, Thorn Carbine, he'd be considered a lazy bum. Any week without a sale was unforgivable, and he'd be singled out for verbal abuse, as would any agent who came in "blank" for the week. He would sooner have stepped in front of a car, than not to have had a sale to report. It was never for the lack of trying, God knows, he was out there pounding the pavement each and every day looking for a lead, and every night trying to make a sale. He'd even resorted to doing it the hard way; knocking on doors. He had been told that once you get the "three no's out of the way, the next door will be a "yes"". But these were hard times with all the lay offs and high unemployment and even that effort had failed.

As Pete started the meeting, Ryker had the feeling that he was about to puke. He knew the drill; after all, he'd been a part of The Rock Insurance Group for over 9-years - ever since General Electric, where he'd worked for three-happy years, before being laid off along with 1,300 other people. He remembered having heard the rumors and knew it was time for a career change, one where he'd be in charge of his own destiny – the captain of his own ship so to speak. At the time, he'd become distrustful of working for another factory – he'd been there and done that, it was time to move on to another type of work.

He remembered an earlier conversation with his friend at the boat club. Ralph was a much older man than he, a jolly man, always laughing, at himself, as he was known to be "accident-prone". Ryker remembered with a smile, that Ralph had often won the "Lose Nut" award, which was given out once a year to the club member who had done the "dumbest thing". One year, he'd forgotten to put the bottom drainage plug back into the bottom of his boat before launching it, and it had sunk at the dock. Another time he'd forgotten to secure the boat trailer to the car, and on the way down the hill to the boat launching area, the boat trailer came unhitched and raced past the car, arriving well ahead of him down near the landing. Luckily, it hadn't hit anyone or thing. During those conversations, Ralph had encouraged him to come to work for him, at The Rock Insurance Company. He had extolled the virtues of the company: great benefits, working your own hours, visiting with and becoming friends with your clients and, therefore, being able to suggest the right insurance plan, tailor-made just for them. So remembering his talks with Ralph, Ryker went to his office and took him up on his offer. In a matter of a few short weeks, he'd studied the insurance laws, passed his state boards and received his license to sell: Life, Health, and Annuities. Later he would pass his boards for all the additional licenses and receive a Broker's License.

At first, the insurance sales business had been a great job. Ryker liked the freedom it offered and felt he was helping his clients to do something for themselves that they couldn't do otherwise and that was to protect themselves and their families from a loss of income or to pay off a mortgage if the breadwinner died and much more.

For a time, Ryker had been very successful, the days flew by, and his family prospered. Then suddenly, the economy slowed and the layoffs started. The newspapers and TV news were all full of doom and gloom; unemployment climbed as factories reduced their staffs, which meant little to no money in the family and the budgets were tightened, and their life insurance was the first to go. The policy lapses were occurring faster than he could write new insurance on new clients to replace the lost commissions, not with standing earning new commissions to pay his bills. It was like swimming against the current while more water was pouring in from heavy rains in the mountains. There was not getting ahead – one was lucky to just keep up with the loses.

It was during the beginning of the recession that their District Office Manager, Matzo Green was pressured into retiring by the Regional Manager, Aaron Long, and a new Manager took over. His name was Thorn Carbine, a short Italian that looked more like a mobster than a District Office Manager. He had been the head of the Pleasantville office, and his badass reputation had preceded him to his new position. He had no sooner taken over than he suggested that Ralph Spinnaker, Ryker's old friend, retire and then brought in his own hot shot from the Pleasantville office, Pete Fordson. Under the two of them, the whole office's atmosphere changed, from people orientated, to sales and profit driven. "Whatever it took to sell policies - do it", became the unwritten business credo. The new philosophy was turning Ryker from an easygoing, happy-go-lucky person into a stressed, depressed and extremely cynical man.

He knew for history how the morning would go. First, Pete would announce changes within the company; new types of policies being offered and any upcoming sales promotions. After that, they'd all get a pep talk that was designed to motivate them to sell a million dollars of insurance in one sale. Oh, yeah, and on the way to the sale, walk on water and raise a few dead people – and if you should happen to raise a dead person, you'd better sell them an insurance policy.

Usually, he had at least one, if not two sales - sometimes, even more, depending on where his clients worked. So when he was screening his prospects, he factored in their places of employment – picking those that had the best retention history. This entailed checking his client's records and then setting up appointments for the next week. After he was done with his office work, he'd take Friday afternoon's off and spend time with his family, working around their home or up in the vegetable garden.

His imagination was boundless when it came to landscaping – it had become a virtual Garden of Eden, so their friends said. He had also taken to writing short stories for the amusement of his children, and for his own relaxation.

He saw that times had changed, with the recession deepening; it made it increasingly difficult to make a sale. Also the change in the company's management style and philosophy, made his business life nearly intolerable.

In mentally reviewing the week so far, two appointments were "no shows" and three others, he couldn't close – they had wanted to "think about it". So, he'd blown it so far for the week. He only had Thursday night to make a sale.

Ryker was also keenly aware that he was well into another poor quarter. If he couldn't turn it around, and fast, his family wouldn't be able to meet their monthly expenses and would be dodging bill collectors for the next three months. He also knew that without a sale for the week, Pete would be going out with him tonight.

Pete acted as if his mere presence would automatically cause clients to want to sign on the dotted line before even hearing about the policy. "NOT". And, oh yes, should they dare not buy, then he'd tell Ryker that he hadn't properly qualified them as a viable prospect. And, if they did buy, and later lapsed the policy - it was still his fault for not properly qualifying them. Either way, it was a no-win situation and everyone hated working with Pete.

He'd heard the other agents, at various times, say that they'd rather quit than to take Pete on a sales call – as you could kiss those clients' goodbye forever. Ryker had already had a couple of his clients tell him, "we like you, but don't ever bring that son of a bitch manager of yours into our home again".

Ryker knew he'd better have at least three, rock solid appointments, or he'd hear about it until hell froze over. In anticipation of Pete joining him, he'd put together a tailor made proposal for each call. If he failed tonight, it wouldn't be for lack of trying. He had lined up three challenging cases with the second call having an aggressive dog. He knew Pete was scared shitless of dogs, particularly if they appeared to be aggressive. Nearly a year ago, he'd tangled with one while out on a sales call with him and it was several months before Pete suggested going out with him on another appointment. He smiled ruefully at the memory, savoring it like a steak grilled to perfection. It was one of the few nuggets of pleasure in his long and distasteful history with Pete.

The two "Ray's": Ray Buckley and Ray Bane, Al Herbed, Ellie Konya, Frank Lopez, Pete Fordson their manager, were already seated, with the Abram brothers being last to join the staff of nine men and one woman. The two brothers were short, husky men who wore designer suits, alligator or snakeskin shoes and smelled of high price cigars, no doubt illegally brought into the country from Cuba by some family member. It was rumored that they were Jewish, which guaranteed them success, as no self-respecting Jew would ever buy insurance from anyone who was not of their culture. He had always liked them and often spoke to Jacob, the friendlier of the two about his family and his business approach with his clients. He was always open to his questions, always giving him his honest opinion.

The face value of the Abram brother's weekly sales was always in the hundreds of thousands, which gave them the status of multi-million-dollar producers at the end of the year. They never missed the "Million Dollar Round Table" Conference, which meant an all expense paid week at one of the top resort areas in the country – so Pete never went out with them. Besides, they wouldn't have permitted it. It was also rumored that they were worth millions, of which most of their money was heavily invested in IBM, Kodak, GE and numerous other blue-chip stocks. And, if that wasn't enough, they were related to several owners of very successful businesses throughout the Triple Cities. Just their presence in the office evoked an air of success and every head turned to watch them as they entered, hoping that some of their aura might encompass them, turning them into super salesmen.

You could have heard a pin drop, as all eyes were upon Levi and Jacob as they pulled their chairs out, momentarily parking their cigars on their engraved, gold ashtrays, and sat down. Every agent on all three staffs secretly wished they could be like them. How did they do it, they all wondered.

Once they settled in, Pete cleared his throat, signaling that the meeting was about to start. He looked much older than he actually was as his face was deeply rutted and scared. Ryker often wondered if it had been caused by some childhood disease, like Chicken Pox. He also knew that Pete suffered from emphysema, a byproduct of his chain smoking, he'd seen it before in heavy smokers. There was always a Winston stuck between his yellow-stained fingers or clenched between his heavily stained teeth.

After Pete completed the announcements, he went around the table, calling on each agent for their new business report. He'd jot it down, making a comment after each report; impressive job Ray; Al, you better pick it up a bit and when Pete got to him, he felt his shoulders shrug, as he simply said, "I'm zip, so far for the week".

Pete looked down his nose at him and said, "I'll be going out with you tonight and we'll get you some business – got any appointments?"

He nodded his head, "Yes", and Pete moved on to the Abrams brothers. He felt like slipping out of his chair and onto the floor under his desk.

Ray, seeing the look on his face, leaned over and whispered, "I know what you're going through, I've been blank week or two over the years, so don't let it get you down. He went on to say, "That if he saw that he was going to have a blank week, he'd fill out an application for a policy on one of his kids or grandkids. For example, a 10K policy and pay it for a few months, then lapse it - just enough to keep old Pete off his back and out of his car". He also added, "the easiest polices to write were term conversions – you know they're already paying for it every month and to convert it to whole life, ups your commission percentage and the difference in cost to them is nominal - so in effect you're doing them a favor. Push the greed button and sell it as a savings plan –

something that they can get back later. Death is always a hard sell, so go with the money, that they're getting back angle – they'll bite every time."

He didn't know if he could do that – selling his kids polices just to look good, and then allowing them to lapse seemed ... dishonest.

He was only half listening, to what Pete was saying, as his last words in front of the staff were still burning into his soul, "we'll get you some business – got any appointments?" He'd said it as if he was going to single-handedly lift him up out of poverty and put him on the glory road. "Just who the hell did he think he was – God almighty?! He was so mad, he'd like to take him out behind the building and beat the piss out of him.

Jacob reported an even 1,000,000 and his brother John, 1,500,000. Pete licked his lips with anticipation of a large bump in his override commissions. Ryker knew that was more business in one week, than most agents wrote in a year.

As Pete looked around the table, he said, "Now gentlemen, you can all learn some lessons on how to sell some real insurance from Jacob and John. What were those policies by the way gentlemen ... Key Man, Partner or Sole Proprietor"?

Jacob and John only nodded their heads and smiled as they got up, and excused themselves, waving at the girls in the front office, as they filed out the front door. Not another man in the office would have dared to leave the meeting before Pete had officially dismissed him.

Once outside, the brothers each got into their new, black Cadillac and drove off. It was known among the office staff, that they had a standing order for a new car as soon as they reached the dealer's showroom and, if not perfect in everyway, they would immediately be returned.

To hear the brothers tell it, they didn't have to go out and knock on doors, the business community called them. Their clients considered it a privilege to have a policy written by either Jacob or John Abrams. It signaled to the business community, that they'd arrived; that they were the elite around town. It was even something to brag about - having insurance with the Abrams brothers.

After taking care of his paperwork, he packed his brief case, got in his old Pontiac 2000 and headed home. He lived outside of Centerville in an area called Osborne Hollow, just off 88, so it took about 30-minutes door to door. Once home, he'd clean up, sit down to an early supper and try to relax for a few minutes, before getting ready to go out for the night. In this business, you never totally relaxed; you worried about where the next sale was coming from. You would find yourself scanning the newspaper for leads: weddings, home sales, the birth list – any special occasion that might generate a sale. Everyone you met at the post office, store, church, weddings, christenings, was a potential prospect or someone who might know somebody you could go see. And, once you had selected a prospect, you did some research, until you knew enough about them to make a call and hopefully, a sale.

His wife, Katie, looked across the table and asked him how it was going. He knew what she really meant, so he shook his head, as he said, "I'm blank for the week, Pete's going out with me tonight – got three appointments, so I'll not be home until late".

Her eyes rolled up in her head, as she groaned, "God, not with him. I don't know how he was ever able to make a living when he was an agent, given his abusive nature". *He remembered that she knew what kind of a man he was, as she'd helped him collect his book, while he'd been laid-up with a bad back for several months.*

He shook his head and tiredly shrugged his shoulders as he chased the last three peas around his plate ... once cornered; he ate them, smacking his lips for the sole benefit of his three children, who had already formed an early dislike for peas.

"Damned, if I know how he did it," he said, as he got up from their supper and prepared to leave.

"By the way, I hear he's also got a young, good looking wife, and I don't know how he did that either," he quipped, as he threw on his heavy overcoat and went out the door, with his wife shouting, "you got one right here, waiting for you ... tonight". He couldn't help but smile at her sudden come back. She was like that, quick with a comeback and as good-looking as she was quick.

Pete was already waiting for him when he pulled up to the office. Pete got out of his car, shut and locked the door, then shuffled over and got into Ryker's. *Pete never offered to use his car and Ryker was just as glad as it smelled like a smoke house in a cold storage meat plant.*

"Where to," Pete asked between coughs, as he lit up again.

"Pleasant Hill, to see Mr. Will Thatcher. He went on to explain that the young family could use a Family Policy. He also knew they had an aggressive German Sheppard, a fact that he didn't share with Pete.

He deliberately parked a good distance from the house, sighting problems with some nails when making his last call here. *When in fact, he wanted to get Pete as far from the car, and as close to the house as possible before they let the dog loose to go pee.*

They got within thirty yards of the house, when Pete started coughing again. The wind was cutting and it had started to snow. Suddenly the door flew open and he could hear the dog's nails biting into the frozen surface, as he lunged toward them.

He heard Pete suddenly inhale as the dog rapidly closed the distance between them, ears back and snarling. From somewhere in the darkness, a voice desperately yelled for the dog to come back. He heard the diminishing sound of footsteps and turned to see Pete hightailing it, full bore, back to the car with the dog in hot pursuit. Ryker didn't know that a man in Pete's weakened condition could run that fast.

Remembering the dog's name, he yelled out to him and extended his hands. The dog remembered him and skidded to a stop, turned, wagged his tail, and trotted over to him. After a few scratches behind his ears, he was soon licking his hands. In the distance, he saw the light come on in his car as Pete entered it. If he'd thought about it earlier, he would have locked it – never knew when someone might want to steal something out of it. *He couldn't help but smile ruefully at the thought.*

Retracing his steps back to the car, Ryker tried to convince Pete that it was okay, that the dog wouldn't bite him. After some conservative movements on Pete's part, his hand hesitantly touched the dog's head without incident. After some more reassurance, Pete decided it was safe to exit the car, and got out shutting the door and walking on the other side of Ryker, away from the dog, back toward the house.

"Why didn't you warn me they had a dog!?" he challenged Ryker, his voice still wheezing from his hasty retreat.

"Slipped my mind," he replied, as they entered the house, just as the dog pushed past them. His clients were all apologetic for the ruckus the dog had stirred up.

Then Mr. Thatcher, unable to contain himself any longer, burst out laughing, "never seen a grown man run that fast – never in my life. I swear to God, you ought to be in the Olympics; you are one fast man".

Before he knew it, the whole house was bursting with laughter, in spite of their best attempts to control themselves.

He knew that Pete was seething behind his hardened smile and, for a second, he saw a glint in his eyes that was as cold as the ice on the Alaskan North slope. *He had the distinct feeling that, if Pete had had a gun, they'd all be dead.*

Rubbing their sides, they all settled down with Mr. Thatcher saying, "Well, after all that, we'd better give these two gentlemen our full attention. After all, we owe that much to them since they were good enough to perform for us – damn, if that wasn't the funniest thing I've seen in a month of Sundays."

After the introductions were finished, he got down to business, first leading in with the problems he saw in their financial picture should one, or both, of them "pass away – God forbidding" and then providing the insurance solution, followed by the monthly premium, quickly calculated by the cost per day as it always sounded better that way.

Apparently, either they felt sorry for Pete or, he had given a good sales presentation, because they bought the policy and we were happy to have found a solution to "their financial problem".

On the way to the next call, Pete went on and on about the size of the dog and how he was sure that it would have killed him, had he not made it to the car in time. He also asked again, why he hadn't remembered to tell him about the dog. This time, Ryker said, he saw so many people, that he didn't remember who had a dog and who didn't, and besides, he knew not to show any dog that he was afraid of them - had Pete "manned up", the dog wouldn't have been a problem. His deliberate jab at Pete apparently worked as he stopped his incessant yapping about it.

It felt good to finally get a sale, but he knew that Pete would tell Joe Carbine that he'd pulled his agent's weenie out of the fire one more time and would take all the credit. He'd also tell everyone how he'd faced down a killer dog to get the sale. *Ryker would later fill the staff in on the real story and, the revised version would give them all a good laugh that would last for weeks.* From that point on, occasionally, one would hear a dog barking as one agent, or another, threw his voice causing Pete to glance over his shoulder with an angry look on his face.

The next client had term life insurance and the conversion was made easier because it had earned some dividends, which he explained would pay for its cost for one year. From that point on, Ryker knew his commission couldn't be pulled out of his paycheck, should the policy lapse.

After that, they stopped off at his last call. The client was either asleep or they were out, as their house lights were off. Pete left a business card, got back in the car, and headed back to the insurance office.

The night was dark and the snow was blowing in all directions, making it hard to see. As he drove along West State Street, he saw a couple of men on his left, walking toward them from under the railroad overpass. They were partly obscured by the shadows cast by the overpass and the snow blowing around the street light. Ryker wondered why they were out walking this late and, moreover, in this kind of weather as there was nothing in the area that would warrant such a late-night walk.

Suddenly, a tractor-trailer appeared from out of a railroad access drive making a left turn onto West State Street, between them and the two men standing on the corner. He hit his brakes to avoid hitting the truck, causing his car to careen to the right.

Pete cussed the man out for his ignorance, as they skidded to a stop, up against the curb on the far side of the street.

As soon as the truck cleared the intersection, they proceeded driving on down State Street, behind him. He had turned his head back momentarily and saw only one man, as he walked back under the underpass, in the direction from which he'd come.

"*Humpf*," he said under his breath, "I wonder where the second man went."

"What man," Pete said, still irritated by the trucker ahead of them.

"Didn't you see the other man - there were two men who approached the corner from under the bridge - and after the truck made the corner, only one man was left and he turned around and walked back the way he'd come. It makes no sense, none what so ever," he said aloud, as his brain kept running in a loop, looking for a plausible answer ... any answer. But none was forthcoming.

"You must have been seeing things - there was only one man," Pete retorted, seemly upset that he was not agreeing with him.

"Well, he knew what he saw and that was it, end of discussion," he told Pete.

Before Pete could argue any further, something went spinning over and over from beneath the trailer and then ended up against the curb, just to their right.

At first, they thought that they were going to hit it, as Pete flinched, anticipating the collision – but nothing happened. They were nearly past it by the time he got the car pulled over and stopped. Turning the four-ways on, he and Pete exited the car, and carefully approached the object. Each of them fearing what they knew must be true. There, lying in a tortured position was what was left of a man. Ryker had to look away as the body was badly mangled and covered with blood. He heard Pete gagging and then he puked and started coughing again.

"That was the second man that I was telling you about – remember?" He said it over his shoulder, as he reached for his phone and called 911.

They waited for the police, and Ryker noted that Pete was uncommonly silent – apparently in shock at what he'd seen.

Almost immediately, they heard sirens, the fire trucks, cops and an ambulance were on the way, arriving in a matter of minutes.

The police corded off the scene with yellow "Police Line" tape, and took a bunch of pictures, as the coroner checked the body. After the pictures were taken, they bagged the body and the ambulance took the corpse to the police morgue for further examination and body identification. They were asked for their names, addresses and phone numbers, questioned about what they'd seen and some notes were taken. There would be more questions Friday morning and an affidavit to sign - for now they were free to go home.

They both nodded and left, anxious to get out of the bitter weather, to the warmth of their homes.

Just as the officer turned toward his car, he muttered under his breath, *"Damn, another one, what the hell is going on?"*

Ryker had barely heard him. What did he mean, "Another one"? *How many others had there been?*

He told his wife what he'd seen when he got home. He still couldn't get the mental picture of the dead man out of his mind.

The Early Morning News was full of the previous night's accident. It seemed the victim in the hit and run was a prominent person within the community. He was on the town board and apparently several other company boards. He left behind a wife and two kids; a 4-year old boy and a 5-year old girl. Momentarily, pictures of the grieving widow and children were splashed on the screen, over a picture of the area where the victim had died.

"*Why do they do that?*" he wondered – *how callus can you get? He bet that if it had been their wife and kids, it would have been handled with much greater sensitivity.*

"*What an awful way to die,*" Ryker thought. *Again, the picture of the two men walking out of the shadows from under the overpass,* invaded his thoughts, followed by the truck coming out of nowhere. *Why had the other man, after his friend had been run over, just turned around and walked back the way they'd come? And, why had he been unhurried, as if he hadn't a care in the world?* Ryker knew he would have been a mess, and would have stayed to help his companion, not turned and nonchalantly walked away, leaving him to die in the gutter.

Then another thought occurred to him ... "*Was this a case of murder that Pete and he had unknowingly witnessed?* That - had – to - be - it ... it was the only thing that made any sense!!

Chapter 2.0

Ryker and Pete were scheduled to meet with the police in their downtown station. They had both arrived shortly before 8:00 am, and, since it was Friday, they had better things to do back at the office and wanted to get this over with as soon as possible.

This time, it was a detective named Jerome Natelli who asked the questions. He appeared to be of Italian heritage with thick hair over the tops of his ears, a Roman nose and dimpled chin, and olive colored skin. He was of medium height, wearing a loose fitting, brown corduroy, suit jacket and leisure pants, which looked like he'd slept in them for over a week, and no tie. He appeared not to be in the least bit of a hurry. He flashed his badge at them from his left-hand pocket, and then pointed to a room off the bullpen.

Aaaah, Ryker thought, the interrogation room. This was where all the magic happened. He could only imagine how many people had spilled their guts in there out of pure fear – some guilty and some not. The detective seemed easy going, until their stories differed - then another plain clothes detective came in and Ryker was asked to follow him.

Ryker was not surprised by this turn of events. He knew from the night before that their stories were different. He had simply seen something different from Pete and now they wanted to find out about that something.

He learned that this detective's name was Harold Scoville and like the first, he also produced a badge, as he talked. He'd flipped the leather case open, allowing only a momentary peek, before it was gone. It was as if they feared someone might read the words and discover that it came out of a Cracker Jack box.

As he entered another small room, Harold motioned for him to sit in the chair on the far side of the table. As in the other room, it also just happened to be facing the mirror – "*what a coincidence*," he thought ruefully.

He knew other detective wannabes were lurking behind the mirror, taking notes about what the witness said and thinking of questions that the interrogator had not thought to ask. Going forward, these points of interest might warrant further investigation.

Absently, he waved in the direction of the mirror, to let the folks on the other side know, that he knew they were there. He knew the people behind the mirror would be somewhat upset by his display of nonconformance - he also knew they'd get over it. His display of joie de vivre was a release from the day-in and day-out pressure he was under. On the other hand, it could be he simply didn't have much respect for them, since he didn't feel that they respected the public in general.

When he was in college, one of the courses he'd taken was psychology and, within these studies, they'd called this form of behavior egocentric. And, it was apparent that the "rank and file" enjoyed their position of importance and their power over the masses by their attitude toward the people they were sworn to serve and protect and for whom they worked. In a word, most of them were bullies, generationally trained by the actions of their parents and perpetuated through elementary and high school by like-minded teachers who were also similarly affected. They found fulfillment in preying on the weak, to build up their own self-esteem.

For a moment, he stared eye to eye at Harold. He was balding, had bad breath and shifty eyes. He noticed that the suit Harold wore, was unlike Jerome's. His was new, neatly pressed and, he wore a white shirt and tie. Hmmm, either he was feeling inferior to his partner and wanted to be noticed as more professional or he had something going on outside of work.

Ryker had developed a sense about people – a gift. He knew if he was wasting his time or not; whether a client would buy or not. He knew what buttons to push to motivate them; there were just three: love, greed and the fear of losing something. He could also read Harold; he was a pretender, playing a part – he was also distracted, agitated and controlling. Ryker pitied his family, if he had any.

Harold's voice broke in on his thoughts, when he said, "I'm ready when you are." His voice was condescending, which Ryker knew was in keeping with his profile.

Again, Ryker told his story: the snow and darkness, the streetlight momentarily illuminating the two men as they came out of the darkness from under the railway overpass and, the truck as it came barreling out of the side drive. *He now thought this must be a maintenance access to the rail yard.* "So why, was a tractor trailer up there at that time of the night?" he asked himself.

"Yes, what is it?" Harold asked impatiently as he pressed the button on his pen repeatedly … click, click, click.

Ryker was also wondering why a tractor trailer would be coming out of a railroad maintenance access at that time of the night, and driving that fast. Also, he would have seen it coming and heard it sooner than he had, unless … it was sitting there waiting."

That must have been it … it was waiting for the men to come into view. When they did, it started up and came rushing at them – only it had hit just one of them. He saw the other man had turned back the way he'd come and had not seemed particularly hurried. As he had thought last night, he would have stayed and helped his friend, not walked away. So, it had to have been deliberate ... a deliberate attempt to kill the man. He must have pushed him in front of the truck. My God, he'd been right, it had been a hit! The full impact of what he'd witnessed the night before suddenly hit him.

"Damn, he was deliberately killed, wasn't he?" His question hung in the air like the pen in Harold's hand." The clicking had stopped and for an instant, he saw something else in Harold's eyes, then it was gone, as Harold quickly said, "wow man, your making a lot of guesses without any proof ... you know, a person could get themselves into a lot of trouble for making unsubstantiated statements like that."

"PROOF - I am the proof! I know what I saw and I saw a man killed on purpose!"

"What makes you think it wasn't an accident?" Harold probed.

Something about Harold's line of questioning and his revisiting the obvious bothered Ryker. He had already lain it out step-by-step – was the man too stupid to follow the logic in what he was saying? Or was it something else? At any rate, he had had enough.

Suddenly he said loud enough to be heard outside of the room, "I WANT TO TALK TO THE CHIEF ... NOW!!" Then, he waited, hands folded, looking at the ceiling.

Harold's mouth dropped open and his pen fell out of his hand. *He had lost control of an interrogation and he looked like a fumbling idiot to all of those who were behind the window. He'd hoped to show that the witness was unreliable – doubting what he'd seen and that his reasoning was flawed - he had failed miserably.*

Ryker heard a thud behind the mirror and a door opening and closing. Then within minutes, their door opened, and an older man came in and motioned to Harold to leave the room.

I'm Chief Myerson he said, as he shook Ryker's hand. I'm in charge around here, so tell me again, what happened.

Ryker threw him an exasperated look, as he asked, "Can't you guys afford a tape recorder?"

To which, Chief Myerson shouted, "SEND IN A TAPE RECORDER".

It seemed like he'd only just asked, when a uniformed cop appeared with one, plugged it in, and left.

It seemed like he'd only just asked, when a uniformed cop appeared, plugged it in, and left. Once again, he repeated his whole story, word-for-word and when he'd finished, he added, "you might want to check the access road to the rail yard, I suspect there's evidence of the truck sitting there for a time, before hauling ass out of there and running over the victim".

The chief, hit the STOP button on the recorder, then yelled, "Send Jerome in here".

As soon as he arrived, the Chief told him to take a team over to the railroad access drive and check for evidence of a tractor-trailer having been parked there for a while, bag it and bring it in ASAP.

"Is there anything else you'd like me to do?" the Chief asked Ryker, as he held up his hand to indicate that he was not ready, just yet for Jerome to leave.

"Yeah - if they find any tire prints, have them plastered. You'll need them for evidence to match with the truck, if you ever find it," Ryker said, flatly, sounding bored. Then his brows furrowed, as he suddenly thought of something else, "Oh ... yes, who was it that got murdered"?

"Beyond that, no, nothing else, that he could think of ... then he covered the mike and leaned in toward the Chief, as he whispered, *"I'd check out Harold's background; bank account, you know, back track his whereabouts over the past few months – he's a little henky, something's not right with him."*

Leaning back, he continued, "In addition, if I do think of something, I'll be asking for you," Ryker added with a wink at the Chief.

The Chief visibly flinched, as if he'd been struck in the gut, but recovered sufficiently to nod his head, as if in agreement, as he signaled for Jerome to leave.

So far, the Chief had been impressed with Ryker's memory and command of details; particularly things that hadn't been thought of by his detectives ... things that should have been checked during investigating the crime scene. But, this last request, by this "insurance man", surprised him – for him to point a finger of suspicion at one of his detectives, was upsetting. He had never felt it necessary to investigate any of them – he trusted his people and there had never been any reason to feel differently. In fact, he felt as if he was betraying a confidence in Harold or any of them for that matter, by doing so.

He waited the Chief out, on his last question, about the murdered man and after what seemed like forever, the Chief, said, "I guess it wouldn't be out of line to tell you, most of the information is already out and his name will soon follow. The dead man's name is Bill Malone; prominent man about town – just got elected to the town board and is currently serving on several other boards, as we find out more information, it will be released to the Press.

With the interview done, at least for the moment, Ryker got up and shook hands with the Chief. He felt that he'd finally found someone who was taking him seriously and something would finally be done.

It still bothered Ryker that the police department operated on such a high-level of ignorance and lack of common sense, no doubt fueled by nepotism. Some people are cut out to be a cop and many more aren't, but along the way, sometimes a cop gets a job cause their brother or dad are cops – a favor here or there owed and paid by hiring the inept.

As he left the bullpen, he had the distinct feeling that more than one set of eyes was following him out of the room and not all of them were thinking friendly thoughts. He hoped that he had not become a marked man for future harassment. He had heard of such incidents from clients who had crossed the police or a specific cop.

Most of the snow had melted and, what was left, had turned to slush as he left the police station parking lot. He hoped that the evidence left behind from the truck had not been compromised – they should have gathered it last night while it was still fresh – it still bugged him that they hadn't. If he'd had anything to do with it, it would have been processed, immediately, while they were working the accident scene. Hell, "accident" my ass - crime scene was more like it. He knew in his gut that this was a murder - the "why" hadn't yet been determined. It was eating at him, and wouldn't stop until he had an answer. He had had enough; his nerves were frayed so he headed straight home where he'd try to relax. But he knew, deep down that his mind never relaxed.

Monday morning he decided to make a quick run into the office and, as he passed through the front entrance, he waved at the girls, wished them a good morning, and went on into the agent's office area. `Only the staff manager had a private office, the rest of them had assigned chairs and desks, which were arranged in a long row, in the center of the room. Each staff had an area within the room, where their desks were also located in rows. Rarely, outside of the Thursday meeting, were there more than a dozen or so agents in the office at any given time and then, only to check for messages, gather sales materials or to check their client's policy records. With these records, they could find out the loan and dividend values at a glance. Often this information was invaluable when it came to converting term insurance to permanent or selling a client a new policy.

He absently wondered where Pete was – probably in with his boss, Thorn Carbine, bragging about his success at saving poor Ryker's week, also he'd claim that he was a key witness in Thursday night's vehicular accident.

Quickly, he checked over the forms for the new policies he'd written Thursday night before turning them in with their attached checks. He wanted to be sure that they didn't have any errors. Next, he tidied up his desk and left, hoping to get back home in time for lunch. On the way out, he overheard one of the girls say, *"Damn we just got another claim on a million-dollar policy written by the Abrams brothers. Doesn't that make three in the past month!?"*

"Yeah, it seems that being insured by the Abrams' is a way to meet your maker," snipped another.

"Now girls," said Susan, the Office Manager, "I'm sure that it's only a coincidence".

"Well, just the same, I'm not asking them to sell me a policy right away."

*   *   *

Not far from their insurance office, behind a stately circa 18th Century home on Beethoven St, a dozen high-end sports cars were parked out of sight behind the home. In the office of this grand old house, sat several well-dressed, older men smoking a pipe or a cigar. The pipes were of the finest engraved ivory and rare burl, filled with tobacco blends imported from India and the cigars were the best Cuba had to offer.

The phone rang; its sound was electronically muffled so as not to irritate the senses and the man sitting at the head of the table.

"Yeah," was all he said as he expressionlessly listened, then he said, "okay" and hung up. He gave no indication to the others in the room about the importance, or lack thereof, of the conversation.

They were all lifetime members of the "Centerville Men's Club". Benjamin Galvani was the President. He was also a multi-millionaire and owner of every McDonald's and Subway in the county, plus a ton of rental real estate buildings. They also had a Vice President and a Secretary. But unlike most organizations who voted on who would hold office, it was determined within this club by who was the richest, and 2nd richest and so on down the line to the last man who barely qualified to be in the club; he was only worth a mere million dollars. You had to have a Masters Degree or higher, an IQ over 120, own a profitable business, and be willing to bend the rules that governed society. In addition, there was another criterion for membership. This information would not be found on any resume and was only known by the people within this club. The final determining factor or qualification was that of accomplishing an assigned hit, which had the appearance of being an accident. In addition, unlike other clubs who existed to help charitable organizations by giving money away, they existed only to make it, and make it, they did. Nothing less was acceptable. Being a member of this club meant security from prosecution and from ever being poor. They had the best lawyers in the world on retainer – lawyers that could and would do anything to win. To ensure success, they had infiltrated the police, city, county and state governments on all levels and owned several judges including a few Feds.

This afternoon, their discussion was about one of their more recent investments, that was about to pay off. The investment model had been in the experimental stage to start with, but had proven to be very effective at yielding huge dividends. The wonderful thing about it was the low overhead and high yields. Since they were in a celebrating mood, a bottle of Chateau Lafite 1865 at $4,650 a bottle, had been brought up from their private collection, deep in the bowels of the house, where neither the light, nor the heat of day could ever find it.

After the butler had poured each of them a glass, he put the bottle within reach of the President's right hand and shut the heavy oak, pocket doors behind him. As he did, each member raised his glass and the President gave the toast. It was short and simple: *"Your either making money or you're not. If you're not, get out of the business."* They all nodded in agreement, as they, raised their glasses, empting the contents with great fervor.

"Now for the business at hand," said the President. We are about to add 3-million dollars to our treasury, at an overhead cost of only 3-thousand dollars and at no risk. Our past investment in the "Three for One" venture has already yielded us over 10-million at a similar cost. I have received orders to widen our venture to include all the areas where we currently operate throughout not only this county, but all the surrounding counties. Give me a show of hands for all of those who wish to continue this journey. All around the table, each member signaled in the affirmative, by raising their hands.

Aaaah, I see that the vote is unanimous – so we will get the ball rolling, using the same model that has worked so well for us to date.

After he'd finished his speech, he waved one of the men over for a private chat. The man was well over six feet tall and built like a boxer. He ran a series of workout gyms, health spas, and aerobic centers all over the Triple Cities and as far away as Stratford. He also had some specialized contacts from the old days, as they too, had a special interest in their model.

The President had heard from "the Boss" that there had been a witness to last night's "accident" and that it could lead to their new business model being investigated – "double check that there is no way anyone can be made". In addition, he was to "lean on" an insurance agent by the name of Ryker Massey, who works for The Rock Insurance Group and witnessed the accident. He has talked to the local police department, and they are listening to his theories.

He had only met the Boss once, when the "Three for One" plan had been proposed to them. He presumed that he lived out of town – which was just as well, as the guy was a sociopath, through and through – he had that look about him that gave him the creeps. He had the distinct feeling that he was very near to being expendable. He waited until after the meeting to have the problem taken care of – to him; it was like having the help carry out the trash – just another box to check off.

Later that night, he made the call from a "burner". "Look Ben, we're having a bit of a problem with a man named Ryker Massey and we need to have him leaned on a bit – give him a good scaring - one that will give him a little message ... like keep the hell out of our business. Maybe an accident of some kind that lays him up for awhile."

Ben was filled in on the logistical details and then the line went dead. He knew what he had to do, but wasn't happy about it – and he also knew that the same fate or worse awaited him, should he fail in executing his mission. He'd gotten the call on a burner phone and, as he walked down the street from the bus station, he tossed it into a trashcan – he had another phone from where that one had come. They were numbered in a series and, after the use of the last numbered phone, he'd been told to get rid of it and move on to the next, in this way he'd never use the same phone twice. He had no way of reaching them – they always called him.

*   *   *

Ryker had spent part of the morning, even though it was Monday, at the office, preparing for the rest of the week. He mostly collected his debit insurance premiums during the mornings and the afternoons he made phone calls, just before the supper hour for evening appointments for the week. He lived and died with each call – praying that they'd allow him to stop by for a "review" of their insurance program, which he hoped would result in a sale.

He'd been giving the insurance sales marketing business a lot of thought. It was getting harder and harder to make a sale of any kind during the recession and keeping it on the books was fast becoming a losing battle. What could he do to fight his high lapse to sales ratio? He knew that because of it, his conservation commissions were in the toilet. What he needed was a product that was virtually lapse proof. In the past, like the other agents, he'd been concentrating solely on life insurance sales for income and it just wasn't enough any more, as he was caught between the near impossibility of making a sale and a high lapse rate after the sale, he knew he had to do something and quick.

As he flipped through the various products, he came upon one that he'd never sold. It had a low commission rate, probably explaining why the others hadn't been selling them. However, it paid a renewal commission every year, and had a high sustainability rating[1]. It was the annuity and it was used for retirement purposes. He grabbed some annuity forms, sales brochures, the product lists from the sales racks and the legal files on it. These he'd use for further study. It looked like he was about to get into the pension business and the best market would be the "nonprofits". With them, he could use the 401K tax shelter as the vehicle for the annuity. There were three major hospitals in the area and a ton of schools, now to find a way to get an employee phone list for the hospitals and schools.

After finishing his morning collections, he was on his way home, and had just gotten on the Towpath, also known as Rte 88, at Chenango Bridge. As he was rounding the last large curve, a tractor-trailer pulled up along side. At first, he didn't think much of it, as it wasn't the first time one of them had been in a hurry, no doubt driven by some 18-wheel cowboy-hauling ass for home or just trying to make appropriate time. Many of them ended up being pulled over by the State Police before they hit Belden Hill. So, he knew that the driver's comeuppance might be just a few miles up the road.

However, this time instead of passing, he drew up even with him and slowed, matching his speed. He suddenly got a sense that something was wrong. As he glanced to his left, he could see that the truck was coming toward him, its duel wheels churning just inches from his side, rear view mirror. There was no way that he could speed up and get ahead of him, as his old car didn't have the horsepower, so he slammed on his brakes, locking them. He could hear his tires squealing as he pulled to the right, to avoid anyone who might be right behind him. The last thing he needed was to have a rear end collision.

---

[1] Once sold, never lapsed

The truck went flying by with the rear crash bar, just missing his left front quarter panel by less than an inch.

He sat for a time on the apron, amid the smell of rubber and the faint sweet smell of oil burning from a leaky valve cover gasket. Wow that was close - too close for comfort he felt, as he fought to control his shaking hands. He knew, had the truck made contact with his car, the resulting accident might very well have sent him to the hospital.

After sitting for a few minutes beside the road to collect himself, he grasped the wheel tightly and signaled. As he looked behind him for an opening, he saw one, pulled out, and then accelerated to match the speed of the traffic around him. He didn't know whether to feel mad because of what had just happened or to be grateful to God for still being alive.

In a matter of minutes, he reached the Osborne Hollow exit and took it. He needed gas, so he pulled straight across Rte 369 and into the gas station.

It was after the 6 pm supper hour, so the rush hour traffic was nearly over, and very few cars were around. As he reached for the gas cap, he could see a car across the street, to his right at the ice cream place and another down the road at the construction yard. Other than that, the village appeared to have been abandoned.

He still felt a little shaky from what had just happened – reasoning that probably the guy was reaching for his paper or something to eat and had pulled the wheel to the right accidently. He was counting his blessings, as he got back on Rte 369, drove under the I-88 overpass, just outside of their little village, and then turned right onto Ballyhack. He couldn't get home soon enough.

It'd been a long week and he was more than ready to relax for the rest of the weekend.

He was relieved to be getting home, as he saw his driveway just ahead. It was carved out of a tree lined, embankment, situated in a shale bottom ravine and as it descended into the forest, it circled and came back to meet itself forming a circle under a dense canopy of old woods growth of beech and oak trees.

Parking the car off to one side of the circle, he got out and stretched. The smell of the forest and the sound of water rushing down the ravine's rocky bottom, some forty to fifty feet below, had a calming effect on his jangled nerves.

Here and there, flowers added color to balance the abundance of the greens of leaves and grass, the grays of tree trunks, and nearly black railroad ties that framed the yard, creating a five-foot high terrace. He followed the millstone walkway across the yard and then to the steps that led up to a huge deck he'd built, the length of their mobile home. He had also built the solar heated pump house, that housed their artesian well.

As he came through the door, he could hear the kids carrying on in the back, and his dog rushed out to meet him. He sat his brief case down by the door, leaned over, and scratched him behind the ears. Thunder was his dog and he always seemed to be able to sense his every mood. When he was home, he was his constant companion – never leaving his side.

His wife, Katie, looked up from the supper she was preparing; her blond hair had fallen forward over the smile on her face, the ends threatening to get into the pot she was stirring. Swatting them back with the back of her spare hand, she asked, "Have you heard anything more from the cops - you know, you did give them a pretty hard time".

"Well, you could say that, but it was a little more complicated than I'd originally thought, and after he'd given her a big hung and kiss, he proceeded to tell her more about it.

When he had finished, she said, "Gee, that Harold guy doesn't sound as if he's too smart – you've got to wonder how he ever made detective."

"I think he's only the tip of the iceberg, when it comes to the lack of intelligence with that bunch - its little wonder that the mafia chose Pleasantville and Appalachian to operate from. Knowing them, they probably have had a hand in who was and is hired, and fired, so they could control the smarts on the force and at the same time keep their finger on the pulse of certain investigations and control their outcomes – pretty sweet if you ask me. In addition, I got to see them in action today, it was like watching an old Loral and Hardy movie. Honest to God, I had all I could do to keep from busting a gut. If I hadn't told them to check for evidence where that tractor-trailer had to have been parked by the tracks, they'd never thought of it. I bet they do find some evidence, like a cigarette or a cigar butt or maybe even a used stick of gum – something that they can get some DNA from that'll match some punk. From him, they can back track and find out who ordered the hit and why.

"Maybe I ought to run for the office of the Chief of Police. One thing's for sure, I'd make a lot of changes in the way they do business and you'd see the arrest rates go through the roof."

"Yes, dear and if I was Ann Landers I'd be giving out better advice for the lovelorn."

"So, what are your plans for this next weekend," she continued.

He knew she was trying to plan ahead – Saturdays and Sundays were the only days they had to catch up around the house and yard." He needed to get a couple of 5-gallon cans of kerosene to keep the hot water heater and furnace going for the weekend - beyond that, he hadn't made any plans. They hadn't been able to afford to fill their 275-gallon tank in some time, so he bought kerosene every few days from the gas station in the "Springs".

For months now, they'd limped along financially from quarter to quarter, each seemingly worse than the last. They'd been forced to drop out of the Boat Club, which they both had enjoyed. Then he had to sell their camping trailer, that had housed them at the club and on the road when they went camping down on Mill Mountain in Roanoke. Finally, he'd been forced to sell the 14-foot run about which he'd bought from his father-in-law and had worked so hard to refinish. Now they were praying that their old car would hold up for just one more week, as they didn't dare ask God for a whole month, and a year was an unthinkable request. It was a weekly event to be taking either the starter or carburetor off and rebuilding them on the kitchen table.

Things seemed to be getting tougher for them by the day and they'd talked about her changing jobs; finding something that paid better, something with a future and benefits, as her current bookkeeping job at the furniture store was only paying minimum wage and there wasn't any medical or retirement benefits.

Katie had heard about a Civil Service Test being held downtown, so she'd made an appointment. The testing was scheduled for the following week – she'd barely made the enrollment deadline. She was nervous about it, praying that she'd do well enough on the test to qualify for the level 5-rating that she was going for and a subsequent open job at the SUNY library. She hated being deceitful, so she only told the people at the furniture store, that she had an appointment in town and wouldn't be in this coming Wednesday.

They apparently assumed she was seeing a doctor or dentist and didn't question her request. She didn't know if they'd pay her for the day off or not and she didn't ask – she hated the thought of missing, even one-day's pay, as tight as things were. However, she dared not miss this opportunity, no telling when they'd have another testing or opening for that matter in the county.

*　　　　*　　　　*

At 15 Henry Street #321, (3rd) floor of the Federal Office Building, Centerville, NY, FBI Director Samuel Ohonahee was hard at work reviewing his many case files – they were piling up faster than he could keep up with them. As soon as additional information came in via phone, email, text messaging, research, or by way of his computer, he'd check it out and, if it was relevant to a case he was working, he'd enter it into the computer system under the appropriate case file folder. When this was completed, all he or anyone else would have to do would be to type in the name and they'd be able to access any information they needed. All this information was stored in the National FBI database - fundamentally in their own "Cloud". This Biometrically gained information came from many sources, from buying property, to renting a mailbox; any information considered to be within the public domain and some that wasn't, like fingerprints, DNA and NGI[2] was available to any agent. Most recently, DNA was being collected from doctor and hospital records and from people supplying it of their own free will, such as on Ancestry.com. As of February 2015 PIA[3], non-criminal and criminal fingerprints had been merged. With each agent, making these respective updates, every field and/or office agent would have immediate access to the latest information on about every person living in this and many other countries.

With all agents and other types of personnel continually adding fresh information to these

---

[2] Facial Recognition – Facebook and Google databases
[3] Privacy Impact Assessment

electronic files, they were being updated in real-time and, therefore, were changing by the second.

For months now, his team had been tracking and building a case. The case file was called "Project Boomerang". This project had grown to encompass interconnected criminal activities in 40-states and many overseas and Caribbean island areas and far beyond.

The DEA, DHS, FBI, CIA, US Marshal Service, Boarder Patrol and all local and State Police, were all involved in following up on leads as they followed the money. To locate the people involved, they were focusing in on enhanced DNA, facial recognition together with filtering all types of communications media and auto scanned license plates.

Director Samuel Ohonahee's (Sam) team was putting in long hours and it was paying off. They'd just tracked some huge deposits being made to a club right here in Centerville, from an insurance company, named The Rock Insurance Group. Given the suspicious nature of these large deposits, this might be the break they'd been waiting for, but first they needed to find more information about this "Club".

With the size of this operation, it was obvious that Sam needed more help – and Albany agreed. By Monday morning, he'd have six more special agents and various support people.

In the meantime, certain information had come to him by way of his informant within the Centerville Police Department BPD, about a suspicious death and he had been told who the contact was – that this might be a lead into a new multi-million-dollar racket. *He wondered if this case and his were connected.*

*   *   *

The phone rang again, at the mansion. The message was brief, "Your man failed to deliver our message." Then the line went dead. The others in the room looked at him for a moment as if asking, *"What is it?"* Subtly he moved his fingers in an outward motion, as if to brush a crumb from his sleeve. It signaled that this didn't concern them - so they went back to playing cards and reading.

He recognized the voice, it was the boss and he wasn't a bit happy, given the crispness of his voice. He took a file out from his drawer – it contained a list of phone numbers. He punched a new number into his phone and heard a voice on the other end, and said, "You failed to deliver, now get the job done or we'll have to terminate our agreement." Then he hung up.

He knew he couldn't afford another bungled job, or it would be he that would be replaced – the insurance policy on him was for 10,000,000.00 dollars and it would only take one phone call for him to become a club asset.

Chapter 3.0

The day broke clear and cold. Not a breeze stirred the dead, snow-laced leaves clinging precariously to the oaks and beech which stood like sentinels around their home.

Ryker rolled over on his stomach – he wasn't ready to get up and face the cold cruel world, at least not yet. A series of loud barks from his German Shepherd suddenly emanated from the front area of the trailer, followed by a series of knocks, that sent the whole house into a frenzy. He couldn't image who could be here so early. It was 9:15 Sunday morning. Well, so much for sleeping in another hour or so he thought, swinging his feet over the side of the bed.

Katie, still in her PJs and bathrobe, corralled the dog into the front bedroom and shut the door, while their three PJ-clad kids gathered in the living room with their noses pressed against the rapidly steaming up windows, straining to see who was there. During the whole ruckus, she was yelling for Ryker, to get up and answer the door.

In a flash, his feet hit the floor; he grabbed his clothes, put on a long sleeve woolen pullover and then a pair of khaki pants, all while propelling himself along the narrow hallway, yelling, "I'm coming." Somehow, he found a spare hand to push his hair down and rubbed his eyes all at the same time as he moved into the kitchen and then the living room.

"God, who in the world would be out and about this early on a Sunday morning," he was thinking, while trying to stifle a yawn. He was already missing

that extra hour of sleep that he had promised himself.

As he passed the window in the hallway, he saw a black suburban parked in the driveway, and wondered how they'd managed to open the metal, cattle gate without getting an electrical shock. He always kept it electrified to keep the bears out and his shepherd in.

Looking through the diamond-shaped window at the top of the door, he saw two men of average height, dressed in suits wearing trench coats. Fed's was the first thing that popped into his mind, as he didn't know any Mafia people ... at least that he knew of.

The dog was still barking and bouncing off the inside of the front bedroom door, anxious to get out, as he opened the outside door a crack – the storm door was still shut, as he asked, "Yes?"

Both men immediately introduced themselves as FBI Special Agents; Samuel Ohonahee and Vincent Rogers and showed him their IDs. This time, he had time to read their badges – he thought to himself, "*Now the real cops have arrived*".

"May we come in?" Samuel asked.

He was well proportioned; obviously worked out, and looked and acted as if he had some degree of intelligence. His slightly wavy brown hair was neatly cut and combed with a part on the right side of his head; a man from the "old school", he thought. He, like his counterpart, wore a three-piece suit, fresh white shirt and conservative, color coordinated tie. Above his left eye was a scar that parted his eyebrow. He also noted that he wore rubbers over his shoes. The other man, who had been introduced as Vincent, respectfully stayed partially behind Samuel; he doubted that either one of them missed a thing, as they took in his home and watched him with a mild smile on their faces.

"As you can see, you have taken me by surprise or I'd been dressed in a three-piece suit and the wife would have just taken a cake out of the oven."

"We apologize for the early hour," ....

"And for not calling, lest you might not find me home," he finished their sentence, with a raised eyebrow.

He enjoyed making them uncomfortable – he smiled as he opened the storm door, pointed at the mat where he indicated they could leave their rubbers. He also wanted them to know that he was in charge here and not the other way around.

He heard the door to the hallway shut and knew Katie had rushed their three children into the back of the trailer for their baths and to get them, and herself, ready for the day. The dog was still growling from the other side of the bedroom door.

Again, they apologized, as he directed them to a seat in the living room and asked if they'd like a cup of coffee.

They both politely declined, indicating that they'd had some earlier. He knew that they would never drink so much as a cup of coffee or eat anything on the job, but he had gone through the formality to be polite.

"So even though I have an idea what you want, go ahead and ask," Ryker, said.

They were silent for a moment, both eyeing him, as they listened to the dog growling in the next room, upset by the tone of his master's voice.

Samuel, as before took the lead, "we want to ask you about the other night, the night of the accident."

Ryker, sighed as he asked, "don't you all work together – I told my story, making it painfully clear to the Centerville cops what had happened.

"So you gave them a statement of fact, about ....." His voice trailed off, as if he lost his sense of direction, hoping Ryker would fill in the blanks.

"Sooooo, it appears you don't know what's going on right under your noses," Ryker said in a voice, appropriately tinged with surprise.

"We're all ears – suppose you fill us in," Samuel said, his voice not showing the irritation he was starting to feel.

But Ryker had noticed ... the veins that were standing out on Samuel's temple and Vincent's clinched jaw, they were called "tells" in the card world. He had them – he owned them.

"Okay, guys," Ryker, now dropped his voice so it sounded like he really wanted to help them, "let's put our cards on the table – you first, so I know whether we're on the same page or not."

Then he sat back and watched them out of the corner of his eye, not saying another word. This was an old trick he'd learned when selling insurance. You make your pitch, seal it with one of the three buttons; LFG[4] that you know will work, then you shut your mouth and wait. *Personally, he liked the love one the best when working with married couples – no man is going to admit that he doesn't love his family, especially his wife ... he's going to say okay, where do I sign, or come off looking like a chump.*

Samuel and Vincent shifted their weight and looked at each other, and then Samuel cleared his throat. *Here it comes – ladies and gentlemen; he could feel the stress they were under, as he knew they were trained to stay in control, that they were the ones who asked the questions.* But, they also knew if they tried to grill him, he'd not be any help to them – he was different – he was like what they liked to see in a recruit, someone who was hard as nails, even edgy and moreover, smart. Therefore, Samuel broke with tradition – he'd give Ryker a little bit, but not all of what they knew.

---

[4] Love, fear of losing something and greed

Nodding his head, Samuel said, "Okay, here it is. First off, we don't work with the local law enforcement until we're ready to spring the trap; you never know who might be an informer. Also, we know that the Mafia is re-entrenched in this area – only they don't call themselves that any more, they're just honest everyday businessmen, as they like to tell it. These so-called businesses are used to cover their real, under the table, money making operations and, besides, it's easier for them to launder their illegal earnings through these businesses. In the old days, it was racketeering, prostitution, gambling, money laundering, dope and selling protection. But, not now – at least not directly. No, they're up to something new – something different and we're going to find out what it is. It's all part of an intricate network covering most every state in the union. In a word, we need your help – we heard that you witnessed a hit and would like to hear first hand from you what happened and any hunches you might have."

"Okay, I feel your pain, so I got nothing to gain by pulling your tails," he said whimsically. So again, he told Samuel and Vincent every detail of the story. Once he'd finished, they were quiet for a moment, no doubt trying to put it together with what else they knew.

Then Ryker, out of the blue, asked, "have you checked to see if there are any other like cases, where prominent business people are getting knocked off, using a truck or some other kind of vehicle"?

Samuel looked at Vincent and he made a quick note. Then they got up, straightened their clothes and shook his hand, thanking him for his help. Samuel handed him his business card, saying, "If you think of anything else that might help, let us know, okay?"

He nodded that he understood, and as they approached the door, Samuel stopped dead in his tracks and asked, "Have you had anything unusual happen to you in the past 24 hrs – *something different?*"

Ryker thought for a moment ... and Samuel seeing that he was coming up empty, continued, "You know that since you're the only witness who saw the whole incident, you are more than likely a person of interest to the syndicate. You do know, that they have eliminated people for less."

Then he remembered the incident the night before, where a truck had nearly run him over. Could it have been an attempt on his life?

Samuel had detected a shift in Ryker's facial expression, and asked, "You're remembering something ... aren't you"?

Ryker nodded, "I didn't think much of it before, certainly not in this context – thought it was just someone taking their eyes off the road for a moment and had been reaching for something...." But, the truck was the same, come to think of it, that I saw run over that guy.

Vincent had his pad out again, making more notes. So, tell us exactly what happened, when and where.

Ryker explained how he'd nearly been crushed by a tractor trailer and now, thinking about it in this new context, he could see how close he'd come to being a statistic. By the grace of God, he had been saved from certain injury, perhaps even death.

"Well, from here on out, you'd better be watching your "six" and we'll be only a phone call away, if you need our help."

He had the feeling that they were giving him back some of his own medicine, which he had earlier, so daftly dolled out to them.

Again, they turned to leave. The movement in the living room, and the door opening again, set off the German Shepherd in the other room. It sounded as if he might come crashing through the door at any moment.

He watched them as they crossed the deck and went down the steps to their car, got in and left. He also noticed that they didn't miss a thing, as their eyes cast about taking it all in.

Did you notice this place, Vincent asked, "it's like a super max fortress and that dog – he sounds like a killer. This man really likes his privacy".

"Well, he does have three kids and lives way out here in the boonies, so I guess I can hardly blame him for wanting some protection, and besides, he's an insurance man and sometimes when your inundated with other people's problems, you just want to get away from it all." Samuel replied.

At the end of the drive, they stopped and Vincent got out and shut the gate, but not before getting an electrical shock that nearly knocked him on his ass.

"What the hell, he yelped". He hadn't noticed the black wire leading from the electric fence, to the steel gate. They'd been obscured by the 6 x 6 railroad ties from the outside, which the gate hung. "Very clever," he thought.

Samuel chuckled, "what'd you get - a wake up call?"

"How the heck did you open it without getting shocked?"

"I used a stick."

"Oh."

"I think we need to develop this source, he's a door opener and can easily work undercover - his job is the perfect cover."

After they left, Ryker sat down for some breakfast with Katie and filled her in on what they'd talked about.

"Don't you think you were a little hard on them?" Katie asked in a weary voice. She'd seen this side of her husband before – where it came from, she didn't know. He could be the most loving adorable man on the earth, and then there was this other side of him; edgy, cold as ice, and sadistically playful with those he was testing to see what they were made of. There would be times that he didn't want to talk – she referred to them as his blue days. She knew he hated his job and was searching for a way out - so most of his moodiness she blamed on his work. She was also working now, so had less time at home – the extra paycheck, was a Godsend.

*   *   *

Ben had been relaxing at the Centerville Men's Club in his favorite place, an over-stuffed chair by the front, 2nd story window where he could see up and down the street. There were only a couple of other members there as most had families and/or grandchildren and, therefore, spent Sundays with them. He had long ago lost his wife. She enjoyed the money he made, but not the hours he spent making it. When she'd threatened him with divorce, taking half of all he had, plus their large palatial home, something snapped. He quickly arranged for a "make up" trip to the BVI and she was excited that he was finally being serious about their relationship. Once there, he'd rented a motor yacht and they'd done some diving. During the last dive of the evening, he'd coaxed her some distance from the yacht and, while diving in a grotto, he'd caused it to collapse, pinning her inside. The coral formations were razor sharp and the slightest touch would cause abrasions, leading to bleeding. He knew the more she struggled, the more cuts she'd get and the more she'd bleed.

He also knew that there were Tiger sharks in the area, as he had sighted them in the distance while they were diving. Now with her thrashing around and blood spreading in the water, they'd be coming from miles around.

Quickly, he swam back to the boat and waited. His story would be that they'd become separated and when he'd gone looking for her, she'd seemingly disappeared. The authorities had believed it.

After an extensive search of the area, they were unable to locate anything and called off the search, never recovering her body. She was designated in their files as missing at sea.

He, of course, went through a period of mourning, punctuated with some heavy drinking, followed with passing out at the bar – it'd worked, as several of the patrons came by, gave him a pat on the back adding their condolences. He'd even gone back with a bar friend or two, to the last location he'd seen her, to see if he could find anything. It had all been for show, but he knew it would play well back at the bars. Everyone would hear the story about the poor man who'd lost his wife and feel sorry for him.

A couple of weeks later, he was back home, where he boxed up all her stuff and, so it would look proper, a month later donated it to Goodwill. After that, his only liaisons with women were those he paid for their services - less trouble and no obligations. He liked it that way.

Accentually, he'd always been a recluse, for as long as he could remember – as a kid, he'd been made fun of for wearing the same pants and shirt every day. They took to calling him rags. He hated being poor – looked down on and scorned by the rich kids. He made a vow that someday he'd find a way to get rich and he did. It started out with studying the stock market, then taking his small savings, and buying penny stocks, then investing his profits in startups, and selling them short and then reinvesting his profits again and again and by the time he'd graduated high school he was well on his way to being a millionaire. Along the way, he started buying up foreclosures and hiring Mexican crews to put lipstick on them – just enough to make them saleable – the ones that didn't sell right away, he rented to college kids. He kept reinvesting his profits until he was a multi-millionaire several times over. But like a drug, it was never enough and then a guy approached him with another type of investment. It seemed harmless – the profits were enormous and all he had to do was front the money. Later when he found out how his money was being used, it was too late to back out – he was threatened with his life. "Shut up and put up," he was told, so he did and, along the way, he got to know who was who and took over. He found out if you can't lick'em, join'em and, as the years went by, he got really good at making the syndicate a lot of money and he was rewarded by moving up within their hierarchy. Now he was next in line to be the regional manager. After their initial meeting, he'd never met him again, but he knew that the boss lived somewhere in the area. He'd only heard his voice over the phone; one or two words and that was it. He was apparently very secretive and very smart.

*   *   *

Thursday had arrived again and thank God, he had managed to dredge up some business; a children's policy for 5,000 dollars, an average size family policy and a term policy to cover a mortgage.

All totaled, it came to 35,000 dollars face value in new business. There was also a scattering of business around the staff – given the 10K that Ray had turned in for the week, he guessed, he must have written another member of the family a policy. As usual, the Abrams brothers reported another couple of million in business, to the applause of the whole staff.

He'd been exploring the pension market. The best vehicle for that was the tax-sheltered program for nurses and schoolteachers. They had a special annuity for that program and he'd learned how to work the government formula for writing 401K tax-sheltered annuities, which would have even better retention. He had also discovered that he had a good market for it with the three hospitals in the area and several schools. Next, he had to develop an "in" and to find centers of influence in which to cultivate this type of business. He was excited about the opportunities and couldn't wait to get started.

Katie was out on the front deck watching the children as they played on the grass below. It had been a good day, as she had received a letter from the state telling her she'd passed her Civil Service test and had been placed at SUNY Centerville in a Level 5 position. They both hugged and kissed – finally they'd have some breathing room.

As she glanced up from the letter, she noticed their German Shepherd, Thunder, was cruising the yard, ever watchful.

Every so often, she'd stop reading and look around; checking the children and to see where dog was, when she spotted a strange vehicle slowly passing their home. It was black with dark tinted windows and moving far slower than the usual vehicles that passed. Even Thunder had taken notice, stopping his sniffing and standing rigidly as his head turned tracking it. In a few minutes, it was out of sight, as it traveled on up the hill. For whatever reason, it made her nervous, so she called the children and the dog in and, as she closed the door, she watched it come slowly back down past their home. Someone was watching them – she had no doubt. Her hands were shaking as she called Ryker.

Ryker, hearing his phone vibrate and, seeing that it was Katie, got up and went into the men's room. He'd already given his report, so there would be no reason for Pete to hassle him. He could hear the panic in her voice, as she told him what she'd seen. He was alarmed to hear that someone was keeping their home under surveillance and told her that he'd check to see if he could find out what was going on.

Hastily, he called his contact in the FBI. "Hey Sam, my wife just saw a black Suburban with tinted windows driving past our home - twice – was that you guys?"

There was a pause, and then Sam said, "No - it wasn't us, though it sounds like it might be a good idea, now that this has happened. We will start keeping closer tabs on you all, going forward. However, we will be using a nondescript car to do it. Is the house above you vacant?"

"Yes ... come to think of it, it is – my sister owns it and it's between rentals. You might consider calling and renting it from her – has everything you need, including a spacious garage. I can give you the number ......"

"Don't bother, we have it," Sam said abruptly.

"Now why am I not surprised?" Ryker replied, his tone unreflective. He now realized that everyone he'd ever known, or used to know, had been checked out to rule out any surprises. *The FBI didn't like surprises.*

*   *   *

Susan had been going over the claim's files – it was part of her job to balance the income (premiums) from the policies and subtract the claims and then check them against the Mortuary Tables[5], then subtract all the overhead expenses, to come up with the profit margin for their office. For years, their regional office had prospered, adding to the company's bottom line, but over the past year, it was losing money. The number of million-dollar claims, versus the number of premiums being paid was killing their bottom line and if it didn't stop, they might have to close the office. With so many million dollar polices having to be paid out, she knew that the home office would start an investigation; something was wrong, very wrong. She sat for several minutes thinking about their losses, and then something occurred to her. Going over to the computer, she pulled up the Abrams brother's business. Primarily all they wrote were term polices with one million or above face values with attached accidental death benefits. What was killing them was that if a person insured with any insurance policy having the Double Indemnity rider and they died by a vehicular accident, or any other kind of conveyance, the policy would pay three times the face value – in other words, "*Triple Indemnity*". So far, the Abrams brothers had written over 20-policies valued at or over one million dollars and over half of them, they had paid a triple indemnity claim. This was extraordinary – unbelievable!

Next, she brought up each policy that the insurance company had paid on, wrote down the names of the insured, each person applying for the

---

[5] Life expectancy

policy[6], phone number, address and beneficiary. It was then that she noticed another commonality. Each beneficiary showed the name of a company; not one was for a family, mother or father. However, she knew that it was not uncommon in cases of "Key Man", "Sole Proprietor" or "Partnership" insurance arrangements, to name a company or partner as the beneficiary. The thinking was that by the company losing their Key Man, whom they had an insuring interest, would cause them to suffer, irreparable damage. The Key Man insurance arrangement was designed to offset the monetary lose to the company for the time it would take to replace the deceased.

She knew that the law was very specific in the requirements for whom you can list as a beneficiary and owner of a policy. They had to have "an insurable interest in the insured and visa versa". Therefore, in this case, since the company met the criteria of Key Man Insurance, they could issue the policy and insure their Key Man, naming themselves as the beneficiary and claim ownership of the policy. The natural progression in her search was to check out the companies who had bought the Key Man Insurance to ascertain who the policy owner and or beneficiary was to be able to pay claims in a timely manner.

Going down the list, one by one, she looked up each company and was startled to see that within a month of paying the claim, each company had gone out of business.

She couldn't believe it – what was going on?! Someone was committing fraud and most likely murder, given the claim dates. *She wondered if any other insurance companies were experiencing the same phenomena.* For that information, she went into the master database and filtered for half million

---

[6] Policy owner

and up claims and found a few in neighboring regions and other companies, but nothing like what they'd been experiencing. Quickly she checked for the names of agents writing this type of insurance and found out what she already knew – the Abrams brothers. No one else in the office wrote that volume of insurance. She knew that the brother's social circle was wealthier and much more influential, consequently, the coverages were much higher. She had not thought anything of it beyond being happy for that kind of business and the money in premiums being paid to the company. However, it appeared that it had led to something sinister and she was momentarily at a loss about what to do about it.

So intent on her work, Susan hadn't noticed that she wasn't alone in the office; that a man had been watching her for some time. He was situated on the other side of the room dividing wall meant to separate the clerk's office from the agent's. The wall consisted of a row of service windows that allowed the agents to conduct business with the clerks. Each window had the ability to be closed during staff meetings to provide privacy. However, one of them had been ajar for some time, but was now closed, and the man behind it had left the office via the agent's door at the back.

A little while later, after making some notes in her "work to do file", and sending out some emails to her superiors, she shut down her computer and locked up. For a moment, she looked at the pictures around her computer and on the wall. One was of her husband that she had taken at their thirtieth anniversary party – he had been a military man, now retired and barely ambulatory. Then there were pictures of their three children; two boys and a girl, all married and with children of their own. She adored all of them.

She slowly got up, stretching her half-asleep legs, and went into the Ladies Room. After washing her hands and drying them with a paper towel, she looked into the mirror. For someone about to retire in a year, she still looked pretty much as she did when she was thirty. She went to aerobics, watched what she ate and was active in volunteering at the local Salvation Army. She wore her platinum colored hair short and in a lose wavy manner, recently styled by a much younger hair stylist than she'd been using in the past. The updated style, complimented her face, making it look slightly longer and, therefore, giving her a much younger look. She also wore stylish clothing that amplified her slender figure.

After leaving the Ladies Room, and the office, she turned the lights off and locked the main door - something she'd done ever since becoming the office manager.

It had been a long day and she was anxious to get home to her husband and fix a late supper. She remembered that on the way, she needed to stop for some salad fixings and beer, as she was out of fresh greens and her husband enjoyed a beer before supper.

She shivered against the frosty night, as she briskly walked from the office to her late model Camry. Since the parking lot was not well lit, she was always a bit leery of what might be lurking in the shadows, so hurriedly entered the car, grateful for the lights coming on. After closing the door, she immediately hit the lock button, and then she took a long deep breath and exhaled, feeling safe within its upholstered steel confines.

Turning the key, elicited the hum of the engine and her radio came on, tuned to her favorite station. Since the parking lot was empty, she put the car in drive, made a "U" turn, entered West State Street and drove toward the North Side Market, where she'd stop for groceries. Frank was usually there to help her with whatever she had to carry out to the car.

In no time, she was back on the road. As she approached the railroad tracks, she could hear and see the lights of a train coming and knew she'd better not risk crossing – she always leaned toward being safe, rather than sorry.

She didn't notice a truck pulling up behind her, as she sat there waiting. She'd been watching for the train, wondering how many engines it had and how many cars were behind it. So much power and sound, it always gave her goose bumps to hear the awesome sound, feel the vibration beneath her and realize the amount of power it had, as she'd watched it go by.

Just as the lights from the train appeared, she felt her car being propelled forward and a terrible sound like she'd never heard before incased her in darkness ....

The train was finally able to stop, nearly a mile down the track. Soon flashing lights were everywhere; ambulances, police, fire trucks, a tow truck, men with flashlights and the heavy rumble of five diesel CSX engines in front of a train that was over a mile long.

There was hardly anything left of the car that was recognizable and the body had to be extracted, a piece at a time by cutting away the steel that was wrapped around it. When the license plate was finally found, the police identified the owner and reported the loss to her family.

The shock from the incident was heard throughout the community like a death knell from a cemetery church bell. She'd been known by hundreds, if not thousands, from near and far. Her family was devastated beyond words, even distant friends wept at her funeral and later at the gravesite.

It was a crowd so large that the police had to direct traffic.

The media reported that the police were vowing to get to the bottom of this heinous crime, as the local press had described it. The public, who had sat apathetically on the sidelines during the recent rash of unexplained deaths, had now come alive – this was someone they knew and loved. It was high time that something was done, starting with law enforcement. They were tired of excuses from an inept police department, riddled with nepotism, which bred ignorance and corruption. Even the Police Chief had admitted, after being badgered by the Press, that they were no closer to solving the murders of several prominent business people and now one of there very own, than they had been back when the first murder had occurred.

The public's temperament was simmering, ready to explode if answers weren't found and soon, and when they did, there'd be hell to pay.

Chapter 4.0

It was Saturday morning. The TV had been full of the news of another death, even breaking into the regularly scheduled programming to give updates of the still unknown person. Ryker could hear Katie bathing and dressing the kids, in the bathroom. Her voice was light and gay as she chatted with their children. The sound lent its self to his lighter mood, after the insanity of this past week.

As soon as he was up and about, he'd turned the TV on, waiting for another update. After hearing that it involved a train and a car, he wondered if it was another one those "Million Dollar Murders". The accident, had grabbed his attention. He had a horrible feeling in the pit of his stomach, that something in his life was about to change – even Katie had become edgy upon hearing the news. He suddenly found himself regretting having turned it on, after seeing that it had caused her happy mood to change to one of sadness.

He'd no sooner finished breakfast, when his phone rang – "can we stop by for a chat?" a familiar voice asked.

"Can't see why not," he answered. He'd no sooner hung up than a black Suburban pulled into the drive.

Putting the dog away again, he opened the door and asked, "Where's the donuts"?

"Oh, was it our turn already?" Sam asked, feigning surprise. It was the first time he'd seen him show any sense of humor.

"Oh, yeah, don't you think," he shot back.

Again, they took their rubbers off and headed for their usual seats.

"Any more visits from strangers or folks in black suburban's like ours?"

"Not that I've noticed," he replied, peering out into space, trying to recall every car that had passed since their last visit. He knew most of them as he was familiar with what neighbors drove which cars.

There was another pause, then Sam broke the silence, "We gotta do some brain storming and figure out just what the hell is going on. Guess you've been watching the news," he injected.

"Yeah, I've been wondering if it's tied to our problem."

"Have you heard who it was?" Sam asked, his voice suddenly very low, seemingly reflecting his sadness.

Shaking his head "no", and with his face down, Ryker listened to what he knew was coming. Sam's voice was barely audible as he spoke, and instantly, he knew that it wasn't something he wanted to hear.

Sam continued, "We just learned that it was your Office Manager, Susan Willis that died in that accident.

He felt his head spin and his eyes blur – "*What ... Susan, it can't be, why he had just said goodbye to her as he'd gone out the door, Friday. What the hell was going on, his mind screamed?*"

He removed his glasses and wiped the tears away with the back of his sleeve. Katie seeing his reaction, immediately rushed to his side with a Kleenex and patted his shoulder, trying to console him. She'd heard the reference to Susan, and had guessed the rest. She remembered that her husband had always spoken well of her.

He sat there for a moment, nodding his head from side to side like a Metronome – "Tick, Tock, Tick Tock," he said softly. It helped him concentrate. When he opened his eyes, both FBI agents were watching him curiously.

Katie explained, "It helps him to relax and think straight."

Smiling, Sam said, "Okay ... you got your clock reset now?"

Ryker without missing a beat, said, "Yep, it's 'time' to get to work."

This time even Vincent smiled, as he reached for his notebook.

"We're going to play a game called, "IF", you ever play that game, Ryker?" Sam asked his eye brows raised, as if he thought he knew something that Ryker didn't.

"Let's back track," Sam said, "from everything we know, which is that she came from her office and stopped at the 7/11, before continuing home. This we know by checking her credit card account, questioning the storekeeper and checking the outdoor cameras to verify the timeline. It seems that she was a regular and the storekeeper knew that she and her husband lived right around the corner – *really nice people*, he'd sadly told them. Also, given that there were no skid marks, we can come up with only two reasons that she got hit by the train. One - she'd not heard the train, since her radio was on and had driven out in front of it or two – she'd stopped and been pushed in front of it. We're going with the second scenario, as from all reports, she was a very careful and very responsible woman who wouldn't have driven through the flashing safety rails. So, going back before she left the office – what, do you suppose she'd be doing at that late hour of the night - any ideas?"

Ryker put his head between his hands and started to put himself in her shoes.

"Well, "if" I were her, I reckon, I'd be checking all the books; new business written, premiums collected, money going out for claims and commissions being credited toward our next quarter. She'd also be looking at other overhead costs. Once she'd calculated all that, she'd know if we were working at a profit or loss."

"Were some of those losses, the million-dollar payouts from your company, for those last murders?" Sam asked.

"Well ... yes, then he continued - since they were all killed by a vehicle, we had to pay the claim on the basis of "triple indemnity" and, as such, it would be three times the face value of the policy; twice for accidental death, plus once for Common Carrier" Ryker said as he rubbed his chin.

"Do you mean by Common Carrier, anything with wheels and an engine?" Sam asked quizzically.

"Yep - or flies."

"Wow, that's a lot of money to be paying out on multiple claims. How many of those can your company pay before they go broke?" Sam asked, as he pondered the financial scope of the situation.

"I suspect that it has affected our claim experience, but all claims are paid out of NEHO[7], so financially it would hardly cause a ripple, but the anomaly would be noticed and questions asked.

"So, who is writing these huge policies, Ryker?" Sam asked, his eyes seemed to be staring right through him.

"That would be the Abrams brothers, John and Jacob."

---

[7] Northeaster home Office

"I think we got enough to get a court order to check her books – I want to know who owns all those policies, the beneficiaries and how many more polices like that are still out there – maybe we can save some people from getting murdered.

Oh, by the way, we have someone keeping an eye on your place and shadowing your family; sure would hate to lose your sense of "time" ... tick tock. He had a feeling that he'd just picked up a nickname.

As they went out the door, Sam asked, "Would you mind going in with us to help go over Susan's records? I think you'd be able to spot something out of the ordinary a lot faster than we could?"

Looking at Katie, he saw her nod that it was okay with her, and Ryker said, "Were good to go".

As he stepped out onto the porch, he noticed a light on in the house next door – so they'd taken him up on his suggestion, to rent it from his sister. Hmmm, these guys don't waste any time, he thought to himself.

It felt good being able to help find the bad guys and to get their lives back to normal.

As they pulled into the Rock Insurance Agency, he saw another black Suburban like theirs and commented about the reinforcements.

"Yeah, we picked up Thorn Carbine, the Manager to unlock the doors and to answer some questions. By the way, what can you tell us about him?"

"He's a first class hard-ass, like his sidekick, Pete Fordson, my Sales Manager. Family orientated and very Italian – wouldn't surprise me if he had some connections in low places."

"Other than that, you love him, right?" Sam said with a grin.

He shook his head from side to side as he wrinkled his nose up in distain, otherwise ignoring the question. He also continued to fill them in on Pete and the other Sales Mangers as they drove to the office. From the voices inside Thorn's private office, he knew that he was still trying to exert his "manager style dominance" over the conversation and by the sounded of his voice, it appeared that he was losing ground.

"See what I mean," he said to Sam as he winked.

The other team had apparently secured the necessary paperwork to gain access to the office records, though he had to ask to be sure – as he needed to cover himself, should the company kick back on his search – after all, he wasn't born yesterday.

"Say, Sam, did you guys get that warrant – I don't want to get fired for being involved in an illegal search."

"Right you are to ask ... yes, here it is," he said, as he reached over and picked up a large legal-size envelope from the counter. It was stamped "LEGAL" FBI, EYES ONLY. Sam opened it and presented the documents to him. "Check them over and be sure our legal people did it right."

Ryker knew that it was more than just a maneuver to put him on the spot, but to show him that they were acting within the law and to see if he could assimilate the legal ramifications.

After a careful examination of the paperwork, he had a better idea about how these things were done; the contents, legal ease and limitations of the search.

Upon finishing, he nodded to Sam, and said, "It appears that they are all in order - though limited to just those items deemed connected with the crime under investigation; fraud, murder, extortion and so on, which are necessary to the extent to support said allegations".

He carefully put the documentation back in the envelope and laid it on the counter, then they made their way into the clerk's office space and he led them over to Susan's desk in the corner.

Sam motioned for him to sit down and, as he did, he noticed two more FBI agents came in and stood by the door. While the door was open, he saw two other agents outside, no doubt charged with keeping the public away. All of them looked slightly younger than Sam and Vincent, no doubt fresh from Quantico.

He didn't know it at the time, but the police had been warned away, as where they went, the press was sure to follow.

Sam hit the START key on the computer and listened to it come to life. He felt funny sitting at "her" desk – someone whom he'd known for years, and who had died just hours ago ... so suddenly and in such a terrible way.

Sam pulled up a chair next to him and Vincent stood, leaning on the edge of a nearby desk.

From the sounds coming through the wall, they were leaning heavily on old Thorn Carbine and Ryker smiled ruefully, as he said, "get him good".

Then he had a hunch, and said, "Susan was the type of person who was the epitome of organization. She lived and breathed it, so I'm guessing she left a report somewhere close by and he started checking the drawers to her desk, starting with the top one. As he suspected, he found what he was looking for - her notes from the night before, neatly typed and in a manila folder, tagged "Weekly Report" and dated.

Removing it from it's envelope, he quickly read it and, sure enough, Susan had discovered the insurance fraud and what she intended to do about it come Monday morning. She'd done her job well in gathering the necessary proof to support her charges. *Only Monday never came for her, but they had.* Shaking his head sadly, he turned and handed it to Sam, saying, "Here's why she was killed - better make a copy of it, so I can put the original back".

Then his mind took off again, as if he was there. "Someone must have been here as she worked and knew that she was doing the books for the month; her financial report and a summation of what was going on ... with attached proof. I suspect whoever it was, will try to get their hands on this report". Maybe you had better have someone or thing keeping an eye on it – just in case.

"Wow," Sam said, as he glanced down through it. Then he started reading it for the benefit of all the agents on their frequency. In summing it up, "here is the smoking gun," he said. "With this information, we are going to track the money to all those who have and would have touched it, until it takes us to the top dog."

As Sam had been talking to the agents through his earwig, Ryker had an idea. As soon as he'd finished, he signaled to him and Vincent to follow him and he led them into the Agent's area.

He deliberately, left the lights out, as he asked if either of them had a penlight. Vincent immediately produced his key chain and on it hung a small LED light. Taking it, he turned it on and slowly made his way down the counter showing the light at an acute angle. At the last window, he stopped, as he'd detected trace amounts of ash lying on the otherwise dust free counter.

"Sam, you may want to take a sample of that and finger print around this window, also the door knob and lock to the back door. If they all match, we have someone to follow to see where he leads us."

Sam immediately started issuing orders and then said, "Impressive job Ryker – see Vincent, I told you he'd be of help to us, so, come on, give Ryker a big hug and a hand shake."

Ryker didn't know for sure, if he was funning with his sidekick, or being serious. He was guessing it might be the former, as Vincent was looking more than just a little embarrassed, as Ryker noticed him shifting his weight from one foot to the other. Ryker, being up to speed, held his arms wide as if expecting a hug from Vincent at any second.

They cracked up as Vincent just kept shaking his head in disbelief.

You know, there's one thing that doesn't jive, Vincent said while still shaking his head, "Why didn't the killer take the notes she'd written - surely he must have seen her writing them?"

"I think that from his position here at the window, he only saw her on the computer going through the books, so thought that once she was dead, there wouldn't be any report. He didn't know she had already written it. Apparently, only I've seen her do it in the past and the killer hadn't.

"Hmmm, makes sense now," Sam replied as he nodded. "At least it's as good a theory as the best we've come up with. Irrespective, I think I'll still leave a team here over the weekend to see if anyone comes back snooping around."

In the meantime, another team of agents had given Thorn Carbine a thorough going over, checking his stories sidewise and upside down, only coming up with his being a mean old man who obviously had no idea what was going on right under his nose.

He gave Ryker a mean look on the way out, that didn't end until he was out the main door. Ryker knew that he hadn't heard the end of this.

Sam, knowing what he was thinking, asked if he needed a note from them to smooth it over.

"Naaa, I don't need a note from mama," he said in a baby voice - that made Vincent smile broadly. "I think he got the message via Fed-B-I," He added.

They were one huge step closer to finding out who was profiting from the "Triple Indemnity" murders. Now to zero in on the insurance agents who were selling those polices – the Abrams brothers.

*   *   *

The Abrams' were sitting down with their extensive family, to enjoy the fruits of their labors, when they heard the door chimes. They were particularly proud of their chimes and would tell anyone who may have commented on them, that they had been imported from England. On the weekends, they set them to chime like those at West Minster Abby.

The butler, had answered the door, and escorted the two men into their presence. Both wore trench coats and looked to be in a hurry. Quickly they identified themselves, as they showed him ID and stated that they were FBI agents and asked Jacob and John to accompany them downtown for some questioning.

Several of the women, expressed alarm at such rudeness and one went so far as to challenge their right to invade their home in such a manner. "Can't you see that we are in the middle of dinner? Have you no common courtesy?" an older woman asked.

The older of the two FBI agents, repeated himself, saying, "That, if necessary, they were prepared to arrest all of them". Jacob and John got up slowly, wiped their mouths and hands on the large lace napkins that had been laid over their laps and left the table. As they approached the two agents, John told his wife to call their lawyer and to get him downtown to the FBI building, immediately. Then they accompanied the agents outside, with each of the Abrams brothers put in separate cars.

Nothing further was asked or said, until they arrived in their downtown offices and were seated in separate rooms. At that time, they were both read their Miranda Rights. An attempt to question them was started, but both refused to cooperate until their lawyer had arrived. All told, he was there inside of 30-minutes, setting a record with FBI headquarters.

Immediately, he challenged them to either arrest them or release them and they quickly reminded their lawyer, one Isaac Shapiro, that they had 72-hours in which to question them, and longer, if they failed to cooperate or, if they were to find they were implicit in a crime, then they'd be formerly charged.

The questioning started after a second lawyer was called in to be with Jacob. The questions were simple to begin with; "What is your full legal name? What is your date of birth?" and so it went, until they started asking the tougher questions.

"How do you meet your insurance customers, you know ... the ones that buy a million or more dollars face value, or do they call you?

"Do you know that the companies listed as owners and beneficiaries are shell companies?"

By now, their lawyers were bouncing off the walls and ceilings, demanding that their clients not answer their questions. However, when the lawyers were shown the proof of this activity, they relented and allowed their clients to answer. Thus it went, until they reached the point where both men were threatened with arrest if they didn't help them get the people at the head of this fraud.

They did learn from Jacob and John, that most of their customers were known through other family businesses. However, most recently, they had been called by strangers to write the new insurance policies; they'd thought this business had come through referrals. No, they didn't know that the companies were shell companies, how could they? It was the job of the underwriters to discover such things. As for the companies that these people were involved with, they appeared to be legitimate; company letterhead, address, phone numbers, business cards – even having an S & P[8] rating. Nothing appeared to be amiss. And yes, to prove their innocence, they were willing to help. They agreed that as soon as any calls came in from people they didn't know, they'd contact them. They also agreed to wear a wire on all future appointments where they were going to write a policy for a million or more dollars of insurance.

They were released on their own recognizance, pending the outcome of further investigations and were ordered to keep in touch daily, reporting their activities. Agents would be checking to ensure they were where they said they were.

So far, things were going well – now they had two men on the inside. The next time these people called, they'd be on top of it, able to shadow the meetings and able to get ahead of these series of events, moving ever closer to those involved in these heinous, triple indemnity murders for profit scheme.

The lab report was back on the cigarette ashes, fingerprints and DNA from the insurance office. The ash type came from cigarettes manufactured by R.J. Reynolds and found particularly in Salem's, Cool's, New Port's, Camel's, Pall Mall's and Winstons. The

---

[8] Standard and Poor's

test group was strongest with the Winstons. There were three men (Ray Thornburg, Al Pittston and Peter Fordson, who smoked Winston's and they all had ironclad alibis – home with their families. They knew that in a court of law that it could be argued that the ash could have been deposited at any time, so it was not overwhelming evidence that could convict any one person, so they dismissed it for the time being.

As for the DNA[9], it appeared to have come from several sources; none were matches for anyone in CODIS[10] or NDIS[11]. What they had, only matched various people who worked or had been in the office for legitimate purposes and all of them had alibis. So, they were back to square one for the time being.

*   *   *

Chief Myerson had heard about an increase in the number of FBI cars in town and wondered what was up. One of his men reported seeing several cars in front of the Rock Insurance Agency. Perhaps they were working an insurance fraud case, since that would fall under Federal statutes. Up to this point, he hadn't been contacted by them and this bothered him, as they usually gave him a courtesy call when working a case in his jurisdiction.

Currently, the only thing he had on the books were three unsolved homicides – he still didn't know the reason for the killings or who did it or why. They had asked the families the usual questions and had come up dry – one of the things that puzzled him

---

[9] Deoxyribonucleic acid
[10] Combined DNA Index System
[11] National DNA Index System

most was that the companies they worked for seemed to have evaporated. He had hoped to interview their co-workers, but this avenue had turned into a dead end. However, he had found some cigarette butts at the location where Ryker had told them to look and were awaiting DNA feedback from the FBI labs in DC.

*　　　*　　　*

The sun had gone down and the streetlights were on, pushing away the gloom that coated the streets in a dull shine. You could tell at a glance that it was cold outside – in-spite-of himself, he shivered just looking at it from the warmth within his deeply upholstered chair.

The house phone rang and he picked it up and said, "Yes". He knew the less he said, the less likely he would raise the attention from those who listened in on all the calls being made these days. "So, tell me what you're going to do to remedy your past sin," he asked so quietly that it was but a bare whisper. He knew that the man on the other end of the line was sweating bullets and no doubt, he was shaking like a leaf in the wind, probably because he too, had a large life insurance policy on him. He was told at the time that it was a fringe benefit for working for them, but now, he knew better. Everyone one in the organization had one, even himself – his boss had made sure of it.

"Tell me what you want, man," the man on the other end of the line whimpered, "and I'll do it."

"Just finish what you started," then he hung up. He felt strangely warm again, his head was clear, as he visualized what was about to happen to one,

Ryker Massey. His man was good at sending messages and yes, he, Ben Calvoni, was good at giving them, he was also good at making money for the organization – better to be an asset than a liability was his main goal in life. One had unlimited benefits, the other was a one-way ticket to hell.

The clock was ticking, sometime within the next 24 hours, the contract would be completed or his enforcer would be eliminated. It was particularly important, since one of his informers had told him that Ryker was working with the Feds and they had all been seen at the Rock Insurance Agency this morning. He knew that all they would find would be records of the insurance policies sold by the Abrams brothers, to various persons working for their many shell companies and from there it would be a dead end. Irrespective, Ryker was becoming a much bigger pain in their ass and he had to be sidelined. It also occurred to him that the FBI might be warning the other insured's, that their lives were in danger. But, so what, the coverage was in force and there was nothing anyone could do about it. The policies were un-cancelable so long as they kept paying the premiums and, at some time, somewhere, the insured's lives would come to an untimely end. Then the policy's proceeds would be paid to the designated and would automatically be sent on to a numbered account in the Caymans. In effect, all their insured's were walking piggy banks, ready to be broken at a moments notice.

Calvoni also realized that it was only a matter of time before they would start using their business model in other places. Spreading the business to unfamiliar places and new insurance companies made good sense with more people to enroll and more money from their premature deaths. He knew that too much business in one area was likely to draw unwanted attention. They could always find eager insurance people in good standing in the community to write the insurance; after all, they'd get a large commission and tons of praise from their managers. It was a win, win, for everyone ... except the well-insured victim.

*   *   *

Peter Fordson had also been taking it easy – his feet were propped up on a cushion, while he watched the football game on his new, wall hung, 60-inch 4K TV. His wife had gone to the kitchen for a couple of refills of their favorite imported beer. They liked to keep it ice cold, so kept a constant supply sitting in a canister filled with ice, while watching the game.

Smoke from his cigarette curled up from the ashtray – one was always lit as he was never without them. His wife, barefoot and wearing only a thong, tiptoed into the Media Room, not wanting to disturb him.

Amelia was half his age and built like a runway model. She was the only thing that could divert his attention from his passion of watching the sports and news – and, at the moment - she was doing a very good job of it.

They'd been married just under five years and had met during one of his management trips – this one happened to be in Toronto, Canada. He liked her right off; she was friendly and smart ... and she was good looking. He knew the look, that unhappy, faraway look. He knew without a doubt that she was ready to move on. He had heard the story before; tired of working the bars and clubs, always hustling for her next dollar and having to worry about her next mark beating her up ... or worse.

So, they'd had a few drinks, maybe one too many, as he was feeling a little cocky ... and, he realized that he wasn't getting any younger. Perhaps that was why he made the move on her; he didn't know at that moment and further, he didn't care. He took her out to eat at a high-class place where he was sure she'd never been and, after that, they had a few more dates, before he had to go home.

That last day, they were sitting in the sun, sipping mixed drinks, when he suddenly said to her, "Let's cut to the chase. I like you a lot and I think you're smart, and a well-put together woman. I also think you want more out of life ... so what do you say about you and I making us a couple and you flying home with me?"

Then, being the master of the sale, he shut up and waited as he watched her eyes – the eyes never lie. As he waited, her face went through an amazing number of looks. For a moment, she looked him dead in the eye, and then she turned her head away and back again. He could tell her mind was weighing all the pros and cons of this new development. Then she looked him dead in the eye again and said, "Okay", I'll give it a go. They were married that afternoon, after they had both picked out their rings. Then they'd stopped over at Niagara Falls for the night and honeymooned all the way back to his home. He had even carried her over the threshold, to her surprise and adoration.

At first, it had been a marriage of convenience, but, as time went on, they fell in love. He knew that she needed space to find what worked for her and he needed space to do his job.

When she first arrived at his home, she was blown away. She was also into him and did what she could to please him. She knew he needed her to be there for him when he got home, from work – the rest of the day was hers; so she'd taken some advanced college courses to round out her MBA, joined the country club where, at first, she was a frequent participant in tennis and golf matches. She was also a frequent volunteer at the nursing home. But still, that wasn't enough, she had long had a latent interest in the Marshal Arts, so had signed up for a couple of courses - one in Karate and the other in Taekwondo. She found the training to be much more fruitful in keep her body trim and hard, than doing Pilates and she was learning something useful. It gave her the self-assurance she'd lacked in her life and a greater sense of discipline. She was always busy, but not too busy to put the time in to her fitness.

On their 1st anniversary, he got her a red BMW convertible. She no longer had to depend on his dated station wagon to get around, and retired it to Don's Used Car lot.

She knew that her husband was doing well, given their very comfortable home and his frequent gifts, but the car was over the top. He was always good to her but, he had one rule: he was opposed to any kind of entertaining in their home. He told her it was because he was a recluse, when he wasn't working. Their home was the one place where he could let down and truly relax. He'd told her that since he dealt with so many people as the manager of a staff of insurance men, that he needed a place away from the public. He had even installed a special security gate at the end of their drive and the place was ringed with a high cement wall and iron fencing – nothing could get in or out. In addition, there was an elaborate, state of the art security system. "It was –

he had told her - *to keep her safe, when he wasn't around.*"

"*But from God knows what?*" she wondered.

Never the less, she'd accepted his feelings and when asked, by her friends, "when was she going to invite them to her home?" she'd beg off saying, "they were redecorating or something was broken and needed repair". She became quite adept at dodging their inquiries.

The only time he'd ever become upset with her was the time she'd stopped by his office to leave off his raincoat. She'd thought he might need it, given that he was going out that night on sales calls and the weatherman was predicting heavy rains. Besides, she'd never met his office staff and the agents he worked with and, thought it was about time she did.

Since the office staff had never seen her, and therefore, didn't know her, she had to introduce herself.

"Hello, I'm Amelia, Peter Fordson wife," upon which they all seemed to freeze in step - one of the women, closest to the agent's windows, got up from her desk and told Pete that his wife was in the lobby.

Of course, all the agents in the room, wanted to see what she looked like, so their heads were popping up like woodchucks in a freshly mowed field. Most of them couldn't imagine who would or could put up with Pete. They were all amazed at how much younger she was and how attractive. They all started speculating on how old Pete had managed to land such a beauty, which ran the gambit. The most popular conclusion being that he had drugged her, got married and she hadn't come to until he had her safely locked away in his home, and then it was too late.

Everyone could see that Pete was visibly upset. His face was beet red and he couldn't hurry her out of there fast enough.

They never saw her at the office again and when she accompanied him on Rock Insurance Company Conferences, he always kept her away from them by sending her on tours, shopping and massages.

Even so, she had started to wonder what was going on and what was he was hiding.

Chapter 5.0

After he left his office, Thorn Carbine was thoroughly pissed. How dare they talk to him like that – who the hell did they think they were? In his mind, they were nothing but bullies. He'd had experience with their ilk in elementary school and later in high school – they were everywhere. At least in college, he'd been able to avoid them by living off campus.

He'd earned his MBA and minored in math, setting himself up for a job on Wall Street but, after a taste of that, he immediately saw that it was a house of cards, ready to collapse at any moment. So, he'd opted to work with a friend for an insurance company. He liked the hours and it seemed like he could make money – as a manager. Not liking the small company pace, he switched to a larger insurance company. For awhile, he worked in Boston for the Rock Insurance Company; they were the biggest and he liked that. Eventually, he put in for a manager's job in Pleasantville where his family lived. He got the job and moved up in the company, as a regional manager. Being a manager suited his nature, as he was over three Sales Managers who, in turn, were over nine insurance salespeople and he had a slew of clerks working for him. His office became one of the best in the country. The home office gave him a call one day and asked him if he would mind moving over to the Centerville office – it's sales were in the crapper and they needed someone, like him, to kick start them again. He felt like a king over his fiefdom. He was there to bring order, unlike his predecessor, one Matzo Green.

Thorn's father had emigrated from Italy, to escape the grip of the Costa Nostra and to make a new life where it was possible to be a success in whatever you undertook. Like so many before them, they had come over poor as church mice. In comparison, they were poorer than a church mouse; at least a church mouse had a rent free heated shelter and they had none. They moved from one hovel to another, to a succession of abandoned buildings, then to charity homes and finally to their own two room cold-water flat. Slowly they worked and clawed their way up the financial ladder until they had a real home and his dad a successful little corner restaurant that he came to own.

In this new business, Thorn had found a safe way of making money, particularly now that he had acquired three handpicked Sales Managers. He had ordered them to push their men to make sales – any who didn't – get rid of them ... one way or the other. Among all his sales people, two men had found a way to sell insurance to some very wealthy and influential people and he was trying to find out how they did it. It seemed that wealth begot wealth and it was their position among their people, which drove their business. Simply put, their circle of influence was at a much higher financial level than anyone else in the office; they couldn't help but be successful. He started encouraging his Sales Managers to canvas and hire people from this upper social class, to stimulate more business like the Abrams brothers. In theory, this made a lot of sense but, in practicality, they found it hard to break into the social circles that operated at that level and find someone who was willing to do that kind of job. They all found out rather quickly, that these people could smell an interloper a mile away and they would immediately shut you out.

Even so, he figured that if he could get in tight with the Abrams brothers, he could ride their coat tails and meet some of their people and find a way in. He even went so far as to buy some life insurance through them to gain their confidence. It worked only as far as meeting their family but, that was as far as it went.

Then something totally unexpected happened – all those million dollar polices, about which they had been celebrating; anticipating years of earning large commission checks, were now having to be paid off due to the policy holders deaths. The claims were coming in left and right for accidental death benefits. Since they also involved vehicles, the claimants not only received the double indemnity amount, but also, an additional amount equal to the face value, known as "Triple Indemnity". NEHO was upset and demanding to know what was going on? Even after today's grilling for several hours by the FBI, he still didn't have a clue as to how or why their million dollar claims were shooting through the roof. All he knew was they had to, somehow, stop the red ink before he lost his job and, with it, his home and his way of life ... at this rate, he'd soon be back to being a "nobody".

*   *   *

With the increased activity in Centerville, the FBI was forced to call in more agents. They'd established contact with all the phone carriers and, subsequently, the towers in the area to track a suspect's phone. They also were using LPR[12] to track movement on the highways, voice-recognition software to indentify suspects, facial recognition software to monitor persons of interest using a little-known software called Tripwire, which had the ability to link all security and traffic cameras in any given area. No suspect, once put into the system, could escape their surveillance.

With the trap setup on their persons of interest phones, they were now able to monitor all incoming and outgoing calls, collecting phone numbers for identification and recording conversations to be used for subsequent interrogation and later at their trials.

*   *   *

Ryker had been warned that there was a contract out on him – it was apparently that he was considered by the Syndicate to be a threat, as he was getting to be to good at what he was doing and he was making them nervous.

Even so, he still had to make a living, so they assigned an agent to "sit on him". In the course of Ryker's workday, he introduced the agent as a trainee to his clients. At first, the man was not very talkative, probably feeling that he was working below his pay grade, but as time went on, he loosened up, particularly when he learned from his boss, Samuel Ohonahee, that Ryker was key to their operations and had been a major help in their work.

He knew that Katie was feeling the pressure. She worried about the children being grabbed or hurt and about him being killed. She prayed that this would end - and soon. Most of all, she prayed for HIS protection over their family. She became super

---

[12] License Plate Readers

sensitive to the slightest out-of-place sound, which would send her running for cover and, she continually watched for any strange cars going by, or on her way to work. She was always vigilant, even though there was an FBI agent monitoring her and their family.

Occasionally, she'd catch a glimpse of the agent and felt better knowing he was there. She referred to him as their personal, in the flesh, guardian angel.

Ryker often caught her breaking down and crying after he returned from work and he'd hold her close, trying to reassure her that things were okay.

Katie was a hard worker and faithful to a fault. She was a city girl, having all that she needed while growing up, where he'd been raised country and poor and they never had enough of anything, but their mother's love. Occasionally their cultural differences caused some friction, but they worked through it. She was high school educated and later, he earned a college degree ... the first in his family. Their children were all in school, so that was a tremendous help, enabling her to work and not have to monitor until they got home. Once they were inside the "compound" their dog became very aggressive with strangers, allowing no one through the gate without their say so. Even her mother and father were held at bay, until they personally let them in.

*   *   *

Alex Thornton was studying at Harvard and had been recruited before he'd graduated. It wasn't unusual for Harvard students to already have multiple job offers before graduating. After making an appointment, he'd met with the AgGIO Corps recruiter in the Student Union.

The recruiter had called him saying that he wanted to discuss a management opportunity. He'd introduced himself as Mr. Frank Forestall. When they met, he noted that Mr. Forestall was well dressed, well spoken and very professional. He was also very intense; his steel gray eyes seem to look right through him. After they'd talked for some time, the recruiter offered him the job. He would be the new Manager of their Agra–Product line, working out of their new Boston Office Building headquarters. However, since they were just getting started, they hadn't finalized all their email, website and other media connections, so getting in touch with them might be a little sketchy at first. If they needed to meet or talk to him, they'd call him.

He went on to say that he'd have complete control over all development and hiring of his own personal staff. They offered him a high six-figure income and he'd agreed on the spot and signed on. He remembered that they had a great health package, 401K and profit sharing and 1/1/2 times earnings life insurance.

Since he was a key man in their operations, they had also insured him for three and a half million dollars, which made sense given his responsibilities to his new company. Almost as an after thought, the recruiter told him that they'd take care of moving him and his family – not to worry a minute about that. The only thing left to do was to have a physical by their company doctor within the next few days and he'd be set to go, when they called to give him his start date. They even made an appointment for him with their doctor, since they had one right here in town, he'd not have to travel far. He'd signed the insurance papers, they shook hands and said their goodbyes.

He immediately called home to tell his family the good news and they were ecstatic for him, but not so much about him having to move so far from his home in Iowa - to Boston, no less, they had lamented.

His dad, James, the careful one who always dragged his feet before finally deciding anything, asked him who it was that he'd signed on with, and Alex knew that he was writing it down. He also asked his son if he'd FAX the company's paperwork to him – you can't be too careful these days, he'd stressed.

He agreed, but not before protesting that he was old enough now to make his own decisions – after all, he was a Harvard graduate, well ... almost, and as such, he should be smart enough to run his own life.

He knew that since his dad was a lawyer and had recently been appointed to a Federal Judgeship, he was very experienced in checking out contracts ... so he let it slide, as he thought, *"Oh, well, let dad spin his wheels, he had better things to do, like getting ready to graduate and party. He also had bragging rights, that he had a super new job."*

*   *   *

Frank Forestall was very pleased with his job as an Upper Management Recruiter. He'd been hired right out of Clemson, before graduation, received orientation along with an auditorium full of other new hires from up and down the Eastern Seaboard. They'd been hired by a new company called AgGIO Corps to fill their upper management tier with capable people. They'd been briefed about the company, how they were to recruit and, about the kit they'd be giving to each new employee. As an AgGIO Corps recruiter, they were given a packet explaining their very liberal benefits package, which included their insurance benefits, pension program and so on.

There was even a policy on each of them, to protect the company from their loss of life. How thoughtful, he thought, that they valued him so highly, as to take out insurance for such a high amount. To top it all off, they also had a contest for the top recruiter, of a hundred thousand dollars. Whoever recruited the most new employees, won the cash.

Now within a few days of being on the Harvard Campus, he'd already signed nine people. It was as easy as shooting ducks in a barrel and the best part was that he was just getting started.

*   *   *

Chief Myerson had been notified by the FBI to turn over all their files on the Triple Indemnity murders and he was not a happy camper. Immediately, he called Harold and Jerome to his office. At first, they thought they were in for a "reaming", given the abruptness of the Chief's request. However, it was an entirely different matter - they were losing control of Boomerang, the case they had started working on some weeks ago. Granted they hadn't made much, if any progress, but now they had to hand it over. Even so, they would still keep working on it on the down-low, even though he knew the Feds could get more done faster with their high tech gear – call it pride or just plain stubbornness, but they had started it and he felt they should be in on it's conclusion.

He shouted, "I want you to make copies of everything you have before we hand it over to them, and we only have a couple of hours before they show up, so your going to need to get right on it. As for the hard evidence, take pictures of it, and be sure to get a receipt signed for each, and every piece of it," the

Chief said, his thick bushy brows bunched into the crown of his nose as if they might meet. With a wave of his hand, he dismissed them.

"Damn Feds, they think they are God all mighty – just step in and take over, just like that," he fumed, as he continued to mutter – "ought to be a law against it. I've seen it happen more than once, over the years – gotta have some Federal pull to do that, you know," he went on, looking around the room for any one or thing to vent his frustration on.

Harold followed along behind him with his head down like a whipped puppy with his hands in his pockets, jingling his keys – he was upset too, but for a different reason. Things were not going well for him. He was the low man on the totem pole when it came to all the Detectives in the office. It had taken him years of walking a beat, and later, finally getting a ride. Then after another year, he'd passed the test for Detective, and had been promoted. But, it was still hard to make ends meet. He had a wife with issues and one of her issues was his lack of financial means to afford her needs. At first, his being a cop was enough for her – it gave her bragging rights amongst her friends, but later, after they'd married, her needs seemed to grow exponentially. They never seemed to have enough money – she'd quit her job as a beautician and now relied totally on him for support. Then the veiled threats started – stories about her friends and how much better they had it than she. They had married good men, men who loved them and took good care of them. Next, she started pointing out other men that she knew she could have with the snap of her fingers. Then she started openly flirting with men, whenever they were out together. It got so he dreaded going home for fear of finding the evidence of another man having been there – later on, she didn't even try to cover it up. He was sick of it.

One day, he'd been sitting in his favorite bar on his favorite bar stool, trying to find a little courage in a bottle of beer, when another man sat down on the stool next to his. There was nothing unusual about that, especially given the hour - many people stopped at their favorite watering hole after work, before heading home. After another bottle, the man beside him made the comment about most jobs in general not paying what a good man was worth. He had absently nodded his head in agreement, as he replied, "Ain't that the truth, especially if you work for the city".

"Awe, you work for the city – that's the pits, only the mayor and her stoolie's make any money in this city. What do you do by the way – me, I'm a salesman?" As he said it, he extended his hand and they shook hands as if they were old friends.

He was now on this third beer, probably explaining why his tongue was a little looser than usual. "I'm a Detective with the BPD."

"Oh, yeah, I always thought they did okay these days, though I hear that some of them work a second job doing security work and what not. Got to be tough anyway being away from the little women all those hours."

"Sometimes that's for the best, when things aren't that good at home ... no more," Harold, said wistfully, his face now a little closer to his half-empty bottle.

"Gee, that's too bad – sorry to hear about that, so what's her problem, if you don't mind my asking?"

He'd taken another long swig from his bottle and sat for a long moment, before replying. Then he said, "money – the lack there of, that is." Then he'd emptied the bottle and signaled for another.

"Well, what if I was to tell you that there might be a way for you to pick up a little extra cash now and then?"

He'd thought about it all the way through the first half of his fresh, ice-cold bottle, and then he asked, even though he already knew the answer, "what are the requirements for such a job?"

"On occasion, I read something in the newspapers and I get curious and want to know more, you know, the stuff that isn't in the papers. No harm done, no one has to know, just stuff to keep my curiosity from running away with itself."

He had thought about it while drinking the remaining half of his beer. *It was true, he could use an extra couple of thousand a month and, from what this man was saying, there didn't seem to be any harm in it. So, the guy wanted some inside information on a case or two – so what, no harm no foul?!"*

Another beer appeared out of nowhere, this time a shot of whiskey was sitting beside it.

He further reasoned that, *"He could always restrict what he sent – only the harmless stuff – and who would ever have to know?"*

He reached for the shot glass and after downing it, took several swallows from his bottle of beer.

"Damn, that was good – been a long time since I was in the Marine's and had a boilermaker," he vaguely remembered saying.

Then he said, to the guy, "what the hell's the harm – sure, give me a call and I'll tell you what's going on behind the walls of justice."

It was then that he turned toward the man and got a look at him. He was well dressed, slightly over six-foot and had a face that looked like forty miles of gravel. He shoved two cards at him, one with only a phone number on it and the other was blank on which the man told him to write his personal phone number and handed him a pen. Again, he nodded as he wrote it down and handed both the card and pen back.

He felt the man's hand take his and shake it and, as he drew it back, there was a thick, folded envelope in it. The man had turned his face toward the bar as he shook his hand. Even in his inebriated state, he thought this was strange behavior. As the man got up, a very lovely lady sat down and put her arms around him and, suddenly, gave him a kiss that he remembered being a lot like the ones his wife used to give during the first weeks of their marriage. Then she got up and smiled, as she walked away. He suddenly had a sinking feeling and, as his hands started to relax, he felt the envelope start to slide – but caught it just in the nick of time, before it fell to the floor.

His head was really spinning as he slid off the bar stool and headed for the back lot where his car was parked. Absently, he shoved the envelope and card into his coat pocket on the way out the back door. He had all he could do to make it to his car – it seemed to keep moving first one way and then the other.

It must have been hours later when he finally woke up. At first, he thought he was home, lying face down on the couch. But, it was cold and something was sticking in his leg and he couldn't move. After wiggling around, he discovered that he was lying in the front seat of his car over the console, his face and shoulders were in the passenger side, while his legs and feet were in the driver's side seat. He had apparently passed out. He had no memory beyond having talked to a man and then a woman having kissed him. He could still taste her kiss on his lips.

After wiggling around, he managed to right himself behind the steering wheel and get the car started – he was freezing. It was then that he noticed that all the car doors had been locked and he knew that was impossible given that the master lock was on the inside of the driver's side door – he wouldn't have been able to lock them given his position in the car. This meant that someone had been waiting for him and dumped him into his front seat, locking the door before shutting it. As he sat waiting for the car to warm up, he could feel something sticking him in the side and feeling for it, found a brown envelop and a business card. Opening the envelope, he could see that it was filled with new 100-dollar bills ... twenty of them by his count and laying beside the envelope was a blank business card, within only a handwritten phone number on one side of it.

Just what had happened, last night? He tried to remember, but most of it was a blur.

Suddenly his phone rang – the number was blocked, but he answered it anyway.

"Good morning, my friend, are you feeling any better?"

He didn't recognize the voice, but felt it best to play along – his head was now thudding with an intensity that made him wonder if he was about to have an aneurism.

"I'm glad you didn't freeze last night – we have mailed a special envelope to your office, to commemorate our new arrangement. Give me a call as soon as you open it, and the line went dead.

"What the hell?!"

"It was already 9:00am and he was late for work. Quickly he called his partner, Jerome and explained his situation. "How about covering for me until I get there – I'll owe you big time – thanks, buddy."

He rushed home, not caring if he caught her with another man or not, he had to get a shower, shave and dress in clean clothes. The house was strangely quiet, as he entered. Looking in the garage on the way through the kitchen, he saw that her car was gone. At least she wouldn't be there to grill him about where he'd been all night. He rushed into their bedroom and noticed the bed was unmade and there were two indentations, one in each pillow. Apparently, she'd had company last night.

Stripping his clothes off, he headed for the shower. It felt good – but it was too bad he couldn't wash away the last seven years of his life, he thought. After shaving, he dressed and even put a tie on, then reached for his badge and weapon.

On the way out, he put his long winter car coat on and that's when he noticed the note on the coffee table. Quickly he walked over to it and saw that it was from Midge. It simple said, "I've moved out, am filing for divorce – you will soon be hearing from my lawyer".

Instead of feeling upset – he felt relieved, like a weight had been lifted off his shoulders. He folded the note up and put it in his wallet – he might need it later to prove that she'd left him and not the other way around – this would give him some advantage during the divorce proceedings, which he knew was coming.

It was a short distance to the office and, after getting there, he asked Jerome if there was anything he should know.

"No, so far, it's been pretty quiet - so what's your story?"

He knew what he meant, so he told him, "Midge has left me, took the kids and has filed for divorce."

"You're shitting me!" Jerome said in surprise. No wonder you're late getting in – probably been up all night hashing it out."

"Yeah, something like that," he mumbled as he set numbly staring at the computer screen.

"Oh, by the way, you got a brown envelope on your desk – came in by special courier – I had to sign for it. It's probably from your wife's lawyer, given what you just told me."

For a moment, he fumbled with it, and then laid it back down – unwelcome news could wait, he had something much more important to take care of, and he hoped he wasn't too late. He called the bank and, after giving the bank teller his social, he asked her to give him his balances. There was a long silence, and then she said, "your accounts are all zero balances, Mr. Scoville. Your wife came in and withdrew all the money – something about our poor service and she would be opening an account at another bank. Since she is co-owner of the account, there was nothing we could do to stop her".

He felt as if he'd been gut punched – his savings and the balance in his checking account were gone. "Damn it," he hissed under his breath.

Recovering, he told the girl, "I want you to open a new account for me and I want her name removed from everything – including the mortgage – do you understand me?"

"Yes, Sir, we will do it right now – again, I'm terrible sorry about this Sir. Please stop in as soon as possible, so that the necessary papers can be signed."

"Yes, goodbye and thanks," he whispered, his voice spent - like his assets.

"I couldn't help over hearing your conversation, Harold," Jerome said. "Man ... she had to have been preparing for this way ahead of time," he lamented, as he shook his head in disgust.

Jerome knew that his partner had been having problems, but he hadn't realized that they'd come to this. *"Perhaps he was better off without her – he had personally pegged her some time ago as a "user". Harold had been doing all the lifting for years now,"* he remembered.

Harold's next call was to HR, where he changed the beneficiary on his life insurance and pension plan to his mother. He told them to remove his wife from any, and all, insurance plans and from his medical insurance. At least he'd save a little by dumping the "family plan" for single coverage. Silently, he thanked God that they'd never had any kids.

Again, he felt strangely free, as he pushed back in his seat, his eyes settled on the envelope lying on his desk and he remembered the strange message on his phone this morning. Slowly he picked up the envelope and turned it over in his hands. He could tell that it wasn't from his wife's lawyer – not yet, and besides, it wasn't the kind of envelope that they used. Theirs would have had their return address stamped on it – and it would have been delivered by a process server. Shaking it, flexing it and taking note of its weight, he had to guess that whatever was in it, was brief and about the size of the envelope.

Pulling the tab, he watched as it cut its way across the flap, causing the brown material on the inside to curl up ahead of the tab. Once it had reached the other side, he reached into the envelope and brought out a shaft of photos and a typed letter – no signature.

As he looked at the contents, it suddenly dawned on him that he had switched from a monkey on his back to a gorilla. The contents of the envelope immediately created a picture of what his life would become. Now, he had a new master. In the envelope were compromising pictures of him taking a thick looking brown envelope from a man at the bar who had his back turned toward the camera. To anyone, looking at the picture, they would easily conclude, that they were seeing a bribe being paid. Also, there were pictures of a lady kissing him at the bar and more pictures of him in bed with the lady – no doubt in some seedy motel, and in another picture, there was money spread all over the bed with them laying in it. If his wife ever saw this, she'd have him by the balls and would make him a financial slave to her for the rest of his natural life. Also, his career with the police would be immediately and irrevocably over. His job was all that he had and now he had a new partner.

Along with the pictures was a business card, with a phone number on it – he remembered that the man had said to call him as soon as he'd opened the envelope. Quickly, he put the contents back in the envelope and then slid it into the back corner of his top desk drawer, as far back as he could reach.

He called the number – it rang three times, then someone picked it up – "it's about time you called – so how do you like the pictures – nice huh?" Without waiting for him to answer, he continued. "Okay, now here's what we want from you ... within the next few hours – send us a copy of the "Triple Indemnity" file and here's the FAX number. Quickly he wrote it down, knowing full well, that right after he sent the FAX, the number would no longer exist.

He knew that every time he did something for them and they paid him, he was getting deeper in bed with them. But, to do otherwise would immediately end his career and put him at a severe disadvantage in his divorce case. As he stood in front of the machine, he weighed the pros and cons for several minutes – then he made his choice and pushed the "SEND" button, and watched as the FAX machine chewed its way through the pages.

At another FAX machine, in another part of town, a man smiled as he watched sheet after sheet pile up in the hopper. When it finally stopped, it contained all the information the police had on the "Triple Indemnity" homicides. Now he'd knew everything the police knew and, he'd know when the police knew it and what evidence they had collected as each day passed.

At the other end of the transfer, Harold put the original file back on his desk – he felt as if he'd just died inside.

But, as he pondered what he'd just done, he started to smile. It was funny how one's enemy can become one's friend in the space of a few hours. He knew one thing, and that was "they" didn't know that there was another law enforcement agency on the case and they were way out ahead of the city police and, to his knowledge, they didn't have a mole on their team.

Yes, the enemies of my enemies can become my friends. He just had a great idea; maybe there was a way out of this mess, after all.

Chapter 6.0

I t was Sunday and Peter Fordson was home pacing the floor in his spacious office. He'd heard about his Manager, Joe Carbine being grilled by the FBI, and his two best agents, John and Jacob being hauled in from a family dinner to be interrogated. He wondered when they'd get around to him. He could just see his income going down the drain, if he couldn't keep the sales going. He needed a certain amount of money to maintain his life style and his wife happy. He was afraid that without it, she'd dump him.

John and Jacob both told him, that they were too afraid to sell anymore Million Dollar Key Man and/or Partnership insurance policies, for fear of being blamed for their client's deaths. They were being called the "Rock's Death Squad" by people outside of the family. Frankly, they told him, that the people were paranoid about being insured by them, feeling that they would be marked men. They were even getting calls from policyholders who were scared to-death of being murdered, and "*to please cancel their policies*". But, since they weren't the policy owners, that wasn't possible.

He was also worried about something else. He wasn't so sure that once the Superintendent of Insurance for New York State, got wind of the number of deaths that he wouldn't decide to suspend the sale of all such polices and delay the payments on those who had already died, until a lengthy investigation had been completed. He had to do something about it before the situation exploded in all their faces.

And, to top it all off, Thorn Carbine had been called and told to come to Boston ASAP, for a meeting with the CEO of The Rock Insurance Company. He had no idea what to expect. *Secretly, he was afraid for his job.*

*   *   *

Samuel had been working on "the board". It was always kept in a conference room away from the occasional visiting media. It wouldn't do for them to blab about what they saw and tip off the bad guys as to what they'd figured out about the Bill Malone hit and run murder case.

They knew who the truck driver was from the DNA off the cigarette butts he'd left behind at the scene and from security cameras located further down State Street. They had also ID'd the truck that had killed Susan Willis, from a couple of street camera's located on the street leading into and out of the crime scene, and again, from the camera's located at the 7/11, before it had arrived at the railroad crossing. However, the man hadn't used the same truck twice. Both trucks belonged to the same fleet located on Upper Court Street. He decided to go look for himself, along with his partner Vincent, and then an idea struck him, to take Ryker along. He had an inborn alertness to things that the others often missed and he could read people with unerring accuracy. So, he had their dispatcher find him and bring him in. As it turned out, he was already downtown in his office, so he was told they'd be by to pick him up, if that was okay. As it turned out, he was bored and looking for a chance to get some fresh air.

On the way over to Tri-Brother's Transportation, they outlined their main goals; locate both trucks, gather evidence, check the lot cameras and, if possible, locate their suspect. The last item was the most important, because, from him they hoped to get a lead on who he was working for and then to work their way up the food chain.

"Guys, we need to ultimately find out who's in charge of the "Triple Indemnity" murder scheme and where they might be operating from. We have six murders that we know of and, surprisingly little to go on, so a lot is riding on finding out something at Tri-Brother's. According to our research, the owner is one Floyd Bergman. He has a clean record – family man with wife and children. Pays his bills on time and belongs to the Kiwanis. His wife is a stay at home mom," Sam said, as he laid the file back down next to him.

In no time, they had arrived and with a warrant, if needed. They pulled up in two cars and parked in front of the building, between two large super haulers. Sam motioned the others to cover the back.

As they moved toward the front door, Ryker hung back, noting who was in the yard, how many trucks and if any were running, where the cameras were located and their collective field of vision.

Sam and Vincent made their way inside with Vincent following just behind Sam. The office was to the right of the access door. The weather outside was damp and cold, so the heat from within was a welcome relief. They could feel and smell it before they entered. The rest of the garage had a heavy oily smell to it. Currently there were two trucks up on lifts being worked on.

Ryker noticed that the ceilings were high, with very little lighting. He watched the two mechanics as they worked; neither of them seemed to be interested in their being there. They probably thought they were salesman. That was good, in case one of them might be "their man".

There were two people in the office; one was a middle-aged woman wearing jeans and a light-colored blouse under an old woolen sweater. She had shoulder length, stringy brown hair, and wore dark framed glasses that made her look like a librarian. She stopped what she was doing, and asked, "What can I do for .....? "

"Yes," the man behind her abruptly said. He was sitting in a large armchair behind an equally large desk and wore a pair of heavily stained bib-overalls over a red, long-sleeved, plaid shirt. As he spoke, he stood up as if to prepare for combat.

Both Samuel and Vincent flipped open their badge covers and introduced themselves.

Samuel immediately asked, "Mr. Pittston, do you know the whereabouts of a man by the name of Benny Barstow?

"Yes, he's under that second truck over there." As he pointed, Riker saw a man bolt toward the door, through which they'd just entered. He immediately turned and stuck his foot out, as Benny ran by, then stepped aside as Benny went face first into the door to the parking lot. Vincent ran past Ryker and pounced on Benny, cuffing him, before letting him up. Then they emptied his pockets and grabbed his phone, putting all his stuff in an evidence bag.

"You got a locker here Benny?"

"Yep."

"How about you lead the way, okay?"

While Vincent was checking out Benny's locker, Samuel stayed with Floyd Pittston, asking him about Benny and the location of the two trucks, having the following ID numbers which he showed him from his notebook.

"Why they're right over there along the fence, waiting for servicing," Mr. Bergman said as he pointed to them.

"You don't mind if we check them for evidence, do you?" He asked Mr. Pittston.

"Nope, go right ahead. Is Benny in some-kind of trouble – gave him a job, hoping to help straighten him out - you know."

"Well, that all depends on what we find."

In no time, a forensics team arrived and started processing the trucks as Benny was being questioned.

They soon learned that Mr. Bergman didn't know anything about his trucks being used in two murders, but he did know a little about Benny's past. He was his Nephew, who had been in trouble; juvie since he was twelve and had served some jail time for auto theft. He'd felt sorry for him and had offered him a job, so long as he kept his nose clean – but murder? It hardly seemed like anything he'd 'be involved in.

His information checked, since they had already read Benny's files.

So far, during the interrogation, they'd learned pretty much the same information from Benny's testimony that they already knew; a kid from the wrong side of the tracks, raised by a dope-addicted mom - after his dad had run off. Boy, if he had a dime for every kid that had sung that song, he would have been able to retire to Hawaii.

Then they asked Benny how he'd started in this "part-time job" and who'd recruited him.

"Well, I'd been out looking at cars in varies car lots around Centerville – I needed a ride really bad to get to and from work, you know. This guy, he comes out of nowhere and we start talking cars - you know, like he was a buddy or something. Kinda just shooting the shit, you know, like good stuff to know about cars. I didn't think not'n of it at first," Benny said, as he tossed his hands into the air.

"Okay, so what did this guy look like?"

"Aaa, I guess middle aged or so – kinda hard to tell since he was dressed for chilly weather - you know with the collar of his long coat pulled up around his face."

"What did his face look like, then?"

"Well kinda rough, like he'd been sick when he was a kid – you know the look – like meat out of a grinder. Oh, yeah, he was a smoker – never stopped."

"Do you know what brand he smoked?"

"Naa ... not in to it enough to care."

"Okay, Benny, what did he say to you next?"

"Well, I kind of settled on a little red Honda Civic – it had low miles and he'd said that it was a good buy and would last forever. But, with my credit in the dumpster and hardly no money, there was no way I could've bought it. But, apparently, he knew it, cause he says to me that he knows of a way that I can get it, and he gives me a hand written phone number on a card – you know, the kind that business men pass out, only this one was blank, except for the number. Then he tells me to call it in an hour, if I really wanted the car. Then he did something that really surprised me."

"What was that Benny?" Samuel's patience was starting to wear thin.

"Well, he handed me a brand-new phone and told me to use it to call him and once I'd used it, he told me to throw it away."

"So, what happened next, Benny?"

"Well, then he walked to the bus stop and got on the bus that had just pulled up."

"And that was it?"

"Like, yeah ... I never saw him again."

"Well, did you call the number?" The FBI agent prompted.

"Well, yeah, wouldn't you?" His mind seemed to drift off...

"So, what did he say, when you called him?"

"He told me that I could have that car and more, if I'd do him a favor, every so often."

"Was the voice on the phone the same one you'd heard in the car lot?"

"Yeah."

"Okay, what else, did he say?"

"He told me to go to the Grey Hound bus station and pick up a key taped to the bottom of seat #13, open the box, read the contents and to call him right back using the new phone number, He also told me to throw the old card in the trash along with my old phone, as the number would no longer work."

"So, did you?" Ryker prompted.

"Did I what?"

"Throw the old phone away?" Ryker asked.

Vincent made a note to be sure and confiscate all of Benny's phones.

"Daa, no, they're too hard to come by – and besides, that's just plan stupid," he seemed put out at the idea.

"So, what was in the envelope, Benny?" Sam continued, his frustration starting to show around the edges of his usually calm demeanor.

"A note, another phone and some money."

"How much?"

"Enough to buy the car."

"What did the note say?"

"The note said for me to borrow one of my Uncle's trucks and to park it in a small lot between the tracks off West State Street. I was to wait until exactly 7 pm, then to start the truck and at exactly 7:15 pm to drive at high speed down the drive, take a left on to West State Street and to take it back to the lot, making like I'd been out for a test ride. And that was it, the note said - simple, right?"

Momentarily, he motioned to one of the lab guys to make a mud plaster of all the tires on both trucks. Then he turned back to Benny.

"Didn't you think doing that was kinda strange for all that money?"

"Yeah, but if that was what he wanted done and there seemed to be no harm to it ... no problem, I'd do it."

"So, you weren't told to kill anyone?"

"God No ... that was an accident, I swear. I didn't find out about that until the next day on the news," and he started to sob. Between sobs he gasped, I'd give anything if it had'na happened – never saw the guy step out in front of the truck.

They gave him a few minutes to collect himself and one of the men handed him a handkerchief.

"Ok, what happened next?" Sam asked gently, his voice reflecting his gentler side, particularly since it was apparent that he wasn't dealing with a cold-blooded killer.

"He called me again after the job and told me to keep my mouth shut about the accident, or he'd rat me out and it'd cost me my job and, as a felon, he said that I'd go back to jail. I was scared shitless."

"Was that all he said?"

"*Well, he did say that if I was ever in trouble, to let him know and he'd take care of me.*" The last statement caught Sam's attention and made the hair stand up on the back of his neck. Now he had an idea how they got rid of possible witnesses and made some money while doing it.

"Did they ever take out any insurance on you?" Ryker asked.

"Well ... yes – said it was a free benefit, so I signed on the dotted line and mailed the form back to them in the envelope they provided. Said if I was to ever die, I get a million dollars – sweet deal, huh?"

"So where did the form come from?" Ryker followed up.

"Well, I got a call, they told me to go back to the Greyhound and under seat 17, I'd find another key and, in the box, would be a form to fill out and some more cash. That's how they always communicate with me. I get a call, and do what they tell me to do." *Sam made a note to have the seats all checked periodically and to review all the tapes in the bus station to see who was leaving the keys and notes.*

Then he had another thought and asked him, "What was the return address on the envelope that you mailed back to him?"

"I don't remember there being any person's name on it or all of the address ... just some PO Box in Pleasantville."

In the meantime, having confiscated all of Benny's phones and sending them to the lab to run traces on all the phone numbers even though they were burners, they were able to zero in on two sets of numbers. Both sets of numbers were incoming from two different phones. Another dead end?! "Damn, it!"

Sam realized the only way this was going to work was to wait until Benny's contact called again and, while he was on the phone, they could triangulate the two phone's signals to locate where the call was being made. Or, if they already had the number they could use Skyhook[13] or Loc-Aid[14] to find the caller's location. One way or the other, they were going to track down who was ordering these hits.

He delayed about asking Benny if he'd been ordered to push a car out in front of a train, not wanting to scare him off from working with them. *The evidence from the trucks would tell them if he was the last driver of the truck that killed Susan* Willis -

---

[13] Skyhook is a mobile locating system
[14] Uses a person's cell phone GPS to determine their location

they already knew that he'd unknowingly killed Bill Malone. The best he would get on that was Involuntary Manslaughter and, given that he hadn't realized that he'd hit anyone, a jury would never convict.

*   *   *

Chief Myerson had been poring over the file, trying to find that one clue that might yield a lead that would break the case wide open. However, no matter how hard or long he looked at it, nothing caught his eye. They had, of course, discovered who the victim was via DNA sent to the State Police Crime Lab and had even questioned the victim's family, asking all the usual questions, but nothing out of the ordinary came of it.

Then something caught his eye. There was a note about a large insurance benefit that he'd signed for – he'd told them that it was a million dollars. It was a benefit provided when he signed on to the board the company, which he'd just started working for. It'd been a new job of only a few days and the family was still waiting for the benefit to be paid, as it would be an immense help in settling his estate.

Picking up the phone, he quickly made a call to Mrs. Malone. She answered on the 5th ring – her voice was weak and sounded as if it was far away. He concluded that she must have been sleeping, even though it was mid-day. He felt empathy for her, as he knew she was grieving. Quickly, he introduced himself, apologizing for the intrusion.

"Mrs. Malone, in our case files, we noted a mention of a million-dollar insurance policy that your husband had on him as a benefit for one of the companies which he had recently gone to work for."

"Yes, that's true – I remembered him bragging about it – saying that he was in the "big time now", with being insured for a million dollars."

"Did the insurance company ever pay that to you?"

"No, we checked on it and they said it was only payable to the company – something about him being a "key man" on their team and the money was used to offset their loss of his services to the company and the cost of finding his replacement."

"Can you tell me who the insurance company was, that had insured him?"

"Why, yes, it was the Rock Insurance Company – some agent from their local office here in town sold it to them."

He thanked her for her time and apologized again for disturbing her, to which she said, "that's okay, I just hope you find out who did this terrible thing to my husband and bring them to justice." Then she hung up. He had the distinct feeling that she was deeply upset by her loss as her voice broke just before she hung up.

Well, at least he had a lead of sorts, now to have his people check it out. Within the hour, they learned that, yes, an insurance policy had been sold out of the State Street office of "The Rock Insurance company, by one of their agents, but the FBI had already investigated their files and talked at length to the staff and sales agents and had cleared all of them of any wrong doing. Even though their information sounded rehearsed, it did give him enough to know who to call next.

As much as he hated to admit it, they were all stumped. Hitting dead end after dead end, just like the Susan Willis case.

He saw the note in the file and remembered having sent a copy of their case file, at their request, on to the FBI - perhaps they'd found something to share.

He knew it was time to connect with his old nemesis. He knew he wasn't getting anywhere beyond knowing who their dead man was, that had been run over by a truck. Other than the two insurance men, one of which had seen it happen, they had no other witnesses. They didn't even have the truck or driver, though they had checked all the nearby truck depots, looking and asking about any trucks that looked as if they'd been in an accident. Zip, nothing ... then he remembered the DNA test that they'd sent to the lab – it should have been back by now.

He paged Jerome and Harold to come into his office. Looking up, he saw only Jerome making his way toward the office. He wondered where Harold was off to – seemed like he was never around when he needed him.

As Jerome entered the office, the Chief asked, "Where the hell is Harold – does he still work for us"?!

"Yes," Jerome said, "he had to run an errand and would be right back."

"The reason I called you in here, is to get an update on the DNA report on the "Boomerang File" – you see anything of it yet?"

"No, but I haven't cleared my "In-File" yet – let me run out and take a look."

Kicking back in his chair, the Chief patiently watched, as his lead detective rushed to his desk and pulled a pile of papers from his In-File and dropped them on his desk, quickly searching through them. Given the depth of his search, he appeared to be well into the past week's mail. Then he saw him suddenly stop and look at a large tan envelope – even from this distance, he knew what it was and yelled, "Today would be good, if you got the time".

Grabbing a hold of the front of his desk, he pulled himself upright in his chair and watched Jerome as he breathlessly reentered the office, tossing the envelope down in front him.

He grabbed it, ripping it open – finally, he'd know who'd been in the truck that had run Bill Malone over, killing him, it was one, Benny Barstow.

"Find that man and bring him in, and don't forget to find out what truck he was driving and get a tech on it – we want every scrap of evidence that they can find. Finally, we're catching a break in this case."

"Yes, Sir and picking up the file, Jerome rushed back to his desk, and did a search for, Benny Barstow. He had a record, but nothing that would indicate to him that he was a cold-blooded killer. He noted his last known address and called Harold, but got no answer, so he grabbed a plain-clothes officer to accompany him.

The house was located off Pearne Street, in the old part of town, where the houses had little to no front yard and were practically touching one another as they stood side-by-side down the long dark, treeless, street.

They found the house even though part of the house number was missing; the porch gave as they walked on it and, when they knocked on the door, the latch came loose and the door opened of its own accord. It became immediately obvious that the house had been divided into two apartments. The hallway smelled of cat urine, to the extent that it burned their noses. Like all the doors, the paint was peeling and, in the case of this one, it displayed two bolt locks. Meaning that it would require two keys to open it – no doubt, a woman lived here and to feel secure, particularly in this neighborhood, she felt that she'd need two locks. After repeatedly knocking and trying the door and it not opening – it appeared that no one was home. They went up the narrow, creaky stairs to the second floor, noting that it must be an attic apartment, giving that the ceiling had a pitch on one side of it.

Again, they knocked and again there was no answer. He must be out. They called in for someone to be sent to sit on the house until someone showed themselves.

He remembered that the records also showed that on a couple of occasions a Mr. Floyd Bergman, had bailed Benny out of jail; just maybe, he'd know where he was. It was worth a try, so he typed in the name on his car computer and found that Mr. Floyd Bergman owned a trucking business and its address.

After driving over, they soon found out that the FBI had beaten them to it by a couple of days and after a quick call to the agents of record, learned that Benny was under their purview, so therefore he was untouchable. They reported back to the office and told the Chief what they'd learned.

"Damn it, they're always two steps ahead of us," the chief yelled, as he slammed his fist on top of his desk.

"Why is it always a matter of too-little-too-late, for this office?" He asked himself. It's always as if they're always one-step ahead of us – then he remembered something that the smart-ass insurance man ... Ryker, had said to him. *"I'd check out Harold's background; bank account, you know, back track his whereabouts over the past few months – he's a little henky, something's not right with him."*

Could it be that Ryker had been right? He shook his head – can't be. He still didn't want to believe it. He'd trained him, and had been his best man. Then he remembered how Harold had gone missing just before they went out to do an arrest or to serve a warrant and the people or persons would come up missing. Seemed like lately he was gone more than he was there working. Even so, he felt like he was stabbing Harold in the back but, with a shaking hand and a heavy heart, he called "Internal Affairs". He reasoned that if Harold was clean, they wouldn't find anything wrong, but if he wasn't – *God help him, because his hands would be tied.*

Chapter 7.0

K atie was in the middle of doing dishes and singing along with the radio. It was one of her favorite Christian stations and it had the best songs. As she sang, her eyes were closed and she was picturing the meaning behind each word, when the sound of glass breaking along with a metallic popping sound startled her.

The children were playing in the living room, oblivious to what had just happened, but the German Sheppard, was up in a flash and out in the kitchen sniffing the air. With his hearing 40-times more acute than those of a human, to him, it had sounded like an explosion.

At first, Katie thought that maybe a bird had flown into the window – occasionally, they'd hear a thump and would go look to find a wayward bird lying on the deck below the window, but this was different, something harder ... yes, much more powerful.

Then looking to her right, where she'd heard the sound, she saw shards of broken glass on the floor below the window and etched in the remaining glass, was a single jagged hole.

Quickly, she ordered their Sheppard back, away from the glass shards, knowing that they could cut his paws. Only briefly did she notice a car drive away. It had the appearance, of having been stopped and then accelerated on down the road.

She rushed to get a dustpan and broom so she could clean up the glass from the floor, before their three rambunctious children could get into it. Then she saw a hole in the side of the refrigerator and, the scope of what had just happened hit her. She screamed and dropped the dustpan and broom. She had all she could do to keep from passing out – the children and their safety were the only things she could think of, as she dove for them, grabbing, and pushing them down to the floor. The dog, seeing her actions, started barking as he raced from window, to window looking out. He sensed that something was terribly wrong.

She punched 911 on her phone; her call was immediately flagged and forwarded to another number and to the phone of the man next door. The signal also automatically went out to the FBI teams. that a team was needed immediately at the Ryker's home. The closest man was already sprinting across the yard to Ryker's home from the house next door.

He could hear the dog barking, as he crossed the open lawn between the two homes. He smashed through the brush separating the two properties, grabbed the top of the post of the high voltage fencing, pole-vaulted over it crossing the yard with his gun drawn and leapt to the deck racing for the door – yelling that he was coming.

Katie yelled back that they were okay, as she put the still barking Sheppard in the front bedroom, and opened the door. As he entered the house, Cal Benson was already relaying the situation over his communicator to the rest of the team.

Katie recognized him, before she opened the door. He was one of the Special Agents that was watching over them. She quickly showed him the hole in the window and where the bullet had entered the side of the refrigerator. She was still shaking – her nerves were frayed from days of knowing that something might happen and now, it had. She needed a release from the pressure she was under – then she saw a female agent among the others pouring out of the Suburban that had just arrived. Shelley Russo rushed into the house, instinctively knowing how Mrs. Massey was feeling – this was not necessarily a part of her job, but, she could relate as she also had a family and kids. Their eyes locked and Katie lost it in her arms. It took several minutes for her to calm down enough to tell her exactly what had happened, though the evidence spoke for itself. Shelley took her statement, as the others went to work on the evidence.

In a matter of minutes, they had calculated the trajectory and had removed the bullet from the refrigerator. Unbeknownst to Katie, they had previously installed two "game cameras" in the trees that had a view in both directions of the road and the entrance to the property. Both memory cards were being reviewed, and filtered by the time of day that the incident had occurred to find the shooter's vehicle. When they had it, the picture was sent to all their divisions; the plate was searched through the DMV, and also their own databases.

Finally, another lead - Samuel was guarded in his enthusiasm, but hoped that it would lead to, not only the trigger man but. to who hired him. They needed to burrow through this elusive maze, to find out who was above these hit men. Who recruited, who trained, who paid and who gave the orders to them?

The plate's owner was identified as Jerry Carsdale. His address was obtained, as well as his last known place of employment and criminal record, all while another team raced to make the arrest.

Ryker had been called – he'd been out working with his clients in the field. He immediately broke off from his work and headed home. He'd been informed of the situation and that his wife and children were okay. Apparently, the shot was not meant to kill anyone, only to send a message. The syndicate was under the impression that Ryker was more of a threat to them than the FBI or that he was the "softer target" of the two.

As soon as he arrived, he rushed to Katie's side, worried for his family's safety. Again, she burst into tears and he did what he could to comfort her. Shortly, she regained control and he gave each of his children a big hug. They were too young to understand what had happened and why all the excitement.

Sam showed him what had happened and told him what they'd discovered and were currently doing. Sam could tell that Ryker was upset, but was hiding it well.

Ryker was mentally analyzing everything he'd seen and been told and was upset that the syndicate would single him out to "send a message". *Really? What kind of a threat did he pose to them? And more importantly, who did he know that would tell them of his presumed importance?* He needed to know more – he needed access to everything the FBI knew ... he needed to see their files.

Turning to Sam, he said, "May I see your complete file on this case – and have access to the war room?" He knew they had to have a board laid out that would give him a visual layout of the players. Seeing it, would give him a better perspective of who and what was involved; who the players were and their subsequent ranking within the criminal organization.

Sam knew that this was an unusual request and against protocol, but he was in charge and, he could say what was or wasn't in their best interest. He was certainly aware of the value of Ryker as an asset, so perhaps it would be best to keep him fully informed of all the facets of the case.

"Okay, Ryker, we'll bring you into our team under certain conditions involving: legal issues, security measures including wearing a bullet-proof vest, protocols, how he was to conduct himself during interviews and what to do if caught in a fire fight. He would also have a special ID and wear a coat like theirs, with the designated FBI/Consultant, lettered across the back.

*   *   *

Two teams had arrived at the residence of the shooter, but there was no vehicle in sight. They quickly surveyed the residence, checking both the front and back doors, while also looking in the windows for any clues or evidence of wrong doing. If they could see such evidence, it would give them probable cause to break and enter. However, they didn't see anything out of the ordinary, and therefore, were restricted to outdoor searches until the warrant was sent. Such documents were now easily transmitted to their onboard computers and printed out, if required. In a matter of minutes, they had it in their hands.

Suddenly, a car rounded the corner and the agents dove for cover, as it entered the driveway. They watched as a tall man in a suit got out carrying a gym bag. He stood for a moment, taking in everything within 180-degrees and as he turned to walk toward the door, it was obvious they were looking at a Special Forces person – there wasn't a doubt given how he carried himself.

They waited until he headed up the sidewalk to the house, before two agents appeared behind him, guns drawn and yelling for him to drop to the ground. They watched him freeze in position. They knew he was mentally calculating his chances of taking them down. But, when he saw two more agents with guns drawn, appear just ahead of him, he knew it was over - so he did as he was told and in a matter of minutes, the cuffs were on, he was searched and then put into one of the agent's cars.

The search yielded a Glock 19, an extra clip, and in his pant's pocket, a money clip containing four thousand dollars, and in his wallet a business card with only one hand written phone number on it, a car registration and no driver's license and in his suit jacket, a phone.

The phone and his other belongings, were rushed to their lab for further study. Sam was hoping that it would yield a list of phone numbers linking this man to whoever had hired him, since he wasn't talking.

With the key and a warrant in hand, two of the agents headed for Carsdale's house. It appeared to be an old colonial, built shortly after the turn of the century. The paint on the steps, hand railing, clapboard siding and flooring was peeling badly. All the wood appeared to be deeply weather checked and the stair treads were starting to rot.

The door was ornately decorated with carved flourishes around the doorknob and a stained window which was coated with several layers of white paint, inundated with years of black soot.

The key slid easily into the lock and the same with the bolt. The door stuck slightly as the lead agent nudged it with his shoulder, forcing it open. The hinges creaked – seemingly annoyed at being bothered.

Once inside, the air smelled older than the house –a good airing out and some new paint were needed. The furnishings were sparse and the house looked barely lived in. Perhaps that was because it hadn't been. The home was owned by some out of town corporation with only two short-term rentals during the past year. As they walked from room to room, they had to push back cobwebs that hung like silk from corners and overhead heating vents. It appeared that even the spiders had given up and moved on.

The current occupant, apparently, had only used the kitchen, bathroom and the living room to sleep in as there was a spread on the couch. The upstairs bedrooms showed no signs of use. After clearing the house, the forensic team entered and started gathering evidence.

Later, after analyzing finger prints from the man they were holding and from the house where he had been temporarily staying, the phone number and the numbers the phone contained, along with the prints from the car, they now knew the man's name and a lot more about him. They also found out that the house was owned by a shell company – no surprise there.

The man's name was Jerry Carsdale, a mercenary of sorts. His only record was for assault and battery – apparently some bar fights. Other than that, it appeared he'd been in and out of the country, employed by different mercenary groups. But, most recently, it appeared that he'd been hired to work for the syndicate. What Sam wanted to know now was what the connection was and what this guy knew about the people he worked for. He doubted he'd ever find out, as these guys had an unbreakable code of silence.

*   *   *

Sam's phone rang and it was Chief Myerson. He wanted to have lunch, today – they needed to talk. Sam had detected the sound of urgency in the Chief's voice, so said, "okay, where?"

"How about Sharky's over on Glenwood, at say, 1 pm?"

"Works for me – see you there." There had never been any love loss between the two and he wondered, what was so important that the Chief would be wanting a pow-wow – maybe he knows something, that we don't, or maybe he's just on a fishing trip. But then, he remembered the sound of the Sherriff's voice and knew it must be important, particularly since he'd never known the old man to swallow his pride and call a meeting on neutral ground.

*   *   *

Pete had been sitting and thinking in his home office for some time. His two best agents and his boss were afraid to write large policies anymore and, certainly, none for a million or more dollars. That meant no more large override checks, a loss of revenue that would vastly affect his business income. He had to do something and do it now.

He called both Jacob and John Abrams to invite them to lunch at the Little Venice at 12:30 pm – "important" - he had emphasized and they'd agreed.

He made it a point to get there early, even after having called to make a reservation, explaining that he wanted a table in the back, next to the wall. He didn't like leaving things to chance, so he'd arrived early to check on the table arrangement, to ensure that it was right where he wanted it. *He hated having people sitting closely around him, when he ate – he also liked having his back to the wall, where he could see others and no one could get behind him.*

They arrived right on time – he liked that about them. Punctuality was a sign of a professional. He immediately thanked them for coming.

He'd signaled the server, when he saw the Abram's arriving, so the drinks were ordered and the menus left behind for perusing. Within a few minutes, the server was back to take their orders. Pete was not without manners, so he'd gone on to ask them, in general, "how they were doing and about their families". He pointed out that soon Jacob's two daughters would be old enough to go to college – which ones had they chosen? Then he asked how John was doing – his family and congratulating him on his son's last football game. "Fantastic catch and touchdown, John, that son of yours can really run – got a little of the old man in him, that's plain to see."

For a time, the banter persisted, and then just before Pete knew they would be served, he paused for effect. Then he said, "Look ... I know you guys have been on edge ever since being hauled in and questioned by the Feds, but honestly, if the best we got in super cops turns you loose, you got to know that they don't have anything on you. And, that's because you didn't do anything wrong! Selling million-dollar Key Man insurance policies is not illegal and guess-what, the company has not banned our sales of it. You can't help it because a couple of your customers got themselves killed. That's not on you. That's completely on someone else – not you, do you understand – not on you, okay?"

He stopped, listened and watched ... waiting for a reaction, as he toyed with his drink. He had thrown a Hail Mary and now it was time to shut up and wait.

He could see that the server was waiting for the cue to serve – but Pete held him off, not wanting to break the moment. Finally, John moved his head up and down, and grumbled, that he guessed Pete was right and then Jacob followed his lead.

"Okay, boss, we'll start writing them again, but you have to promise to back us and tell the people we are not to blame for a few unlucky people getting themselves killed. That's not on us.

Pete nodded his head and agreed to be sure everyone in the range of his voice understood as he signaled to the server that they were ready to eat. Jacob and John seemed to be pleased with his support and dug into their hot lunch.

After the meal, Pete headed to the Rock Insurance Company's office. He wanted to catch Thorn before he left for the day. He knocked on his door before entering and caught him catching a few ZZZs.

He knew Thorn was embarrassed, feeling that it was important to always act in a professional manner while doing the company's business. Therefore, Pete knew Thorn would be in his debt for keeping his little secret and therefore, would be more cooperative.

Quickly, he appraised Thorn of his conversation with the Abrams brothers. In addition, how they'd agreed to continue selling Key Man and Partnership insurance. Even though he was excited, it didn't seem to convey to Thorn.

"I got to tell you Pete, it's getting pretty hot in the kitchen and I got to wonder if it wouldn't be just as wise to just let go of that wild cat for awhile."

"Look, if we were doing anything wrong, the Feds would have us all in jail, but there's no connection between our legally selling insurance and what's happening to a few of our insured's. If anything was going on, you can bet the farm that our company would not be issuing the policies.

He watched as Thorn rubbed his chin, then shook his head. He then reluctantly said, "Okay, your right – got to wrap up here and get out of this office before I go crazy. Have a good night, Pete."

It was well into the week and he wondered how the rest of his staff was doing. He was secretly hoping that the Abrams brothers would be bringing in more of their key man policies – he needed it.

*   *   *

The phone, which was sitting on the edge of the table, rang in the upstairs conference room. Its tone was subtle, hardly audible and a hand with a large diamond ring on the pinky finger, reached for it. Ben had been sitting in his recliner watching the traffic passing below and, in particular, an attractive young woman that happened to be standing on the street corner waiting for a break in the traffic before crossing. He'd seen her about this time every day, so he knew she worked and lived somewhere between these two points. He desired to know more about her; who she was, where she worked and lived – he wanted to get to know her – perhaps they might have an *affaire romantique.*

His gaze was forced to break away to see who was calling. All irritation disappeared as the voice on the other end of the line said, "Hello, Ben, I want you to speed up our business." Then the line went dead.

It was the boss and the sound of his voice made him remember just how minuscule he really was in the grand scheme of things.

*   *   *

Ryker stopped into his insurance office and saw Ray sitting at his desk, which was situated next to his. Usually, he rarely saw him come in and, if he did, it was only briefly as he grabbed some sales brochures and worksheets and was gone again.

As he sat down, Ray leaned over ever so slightly and whispered – "don't look at me, but make like you're just doing your paper work – got something to tell you.

"Okay, he whispered, as he removed some papers from his briefcase and pretended to be reading them.

"Ryker, I've been here for nearly 20-years – looking at retiring as soon as I can. This used to be a great place to work, before that son of a bitch, Pete took over – they're pressuring me to retire early, even though they know that I'll lose over 75 percent of my pension if I do."

"Why – how can they do that?"

"Why ... cause, they don't want to pay me my full benefit - that's why." He could feel the pain and frustration in Ray's voice.

"You might want to watch your back, too, as I've seen Pete around town, at various restaurants, talking to young people. I think he's out recruiting some new agents."

Ryker knew that he was not exactly setting the world on fire, but he had discovered a new type of policy to sell and he had been calling a few nurses and teachers for the past few weeks, setting up appointments. He'd even gone so far as to buy a special calculator that he had previously programmed to do the complicated formulas.

He also knew that next to their previous boss, a saint of a man, this one was the reincarnation of Captain Bligh.

"Thanks for the heads up, Ray. Let me know if you'd like some sales leads."

Then as an after thought, Ryker ask him, "You don't happen to know where Pete lives do you - he happened to stop there one night, we parked on the road, he told me to stay in the car until he got back – never invited me in. I thought that was kinda strange."

"Yeah, he has moments – lives in a gated mansion on top of the mountain over looking 17 and 81, frankly, *I don't know how he affords the place.*" After writing the address down, he handed him a yellow stick-up.

"Okay - gotta run, don't want "him" catching me here."

Out of the corner of his eye, Ryker watched him, hurriedly leave.

He had a feeling that everyone on the staff disliked Pete and wished they could be reassigned, even if it meant Pleasantville or Hill Valley. Even he'd considered it as a real possibility. In ten years he'd have his vested rights to a small pension when he turned 65, which seemed like light years from now.

*   *   *

The phone rang on the desk of Samuel Ohonahee as his phone vibrated in his pocket. He was currently in a meeting with his staff in the war room. Then his phone suddenly stopped vibrating, followed by a timid knock on the door. Their Office Manager stuck her head in saying, "It's very important, he wants to talk only to you, Mr. Ohonahee."

"Who is it?" Sam asked impatiently.

"It's a Mr. Harold Scoville, a Detective from the Centerville Police Department - says that he needs to talk to you ASAP ... *that it's a matter of life and death.*

Chapter 8.0

Alex's phone was ringing somewhere under his shirt and pants, where he'd thrown them on the couch. He'd been out running and, as soon as his door shut, he started stripping as he headed for the shower, where the sound of water splashing in the shower door further deaden the sound of the phone's ringing.

It'd been a busy few days with the new job, having a physical, preparing for finals, partying and saying goodbye to his friends. He'd been looking forward to his morning run to help clear his mind and now he was in a rush to meet Lexi, his girlfriend. She was very special to him and he couldn't wait for her to meet his family, particularly since they'd been going together long enough to be reasonably sure he wouldn't lose her afterwards.

He recalled the last time he'd taken a girl friend home and afterwards she'd bolted – they were way to much for her. Only through epic maneuvering, had he been able to keep Lexi under wraps, away from his parents these past two years. He hoped to spare her until he'd sufficiently warned her about them. He knew how they'd be - mom would want to know all about her family – the whole pedigree and would interrogate her like a Gestapo Field Marshal. His dad would be antisocial until his mother approved, and then he'd communicate using only three to four-word sentences all in the first person, active voice, while looking owlishly over his half lens glasses, as if he was examining a bug.

They had decided to meet at 7 pm at the Grafton Street Pub & Grill, located at Harvard Square. It had a Mediterranean feel that they loved and, with the outdoor wrought iron tables and chairs, it was perfect. Whenever they went there, they always shared their favorite, Powers Irish coffee ... it was all a slice of heaven. He'd called right after making their plans and had secured, a hard to get, reservation. As he put on a black polo shirt over a pair of white yachting pants, he was already anticipating seeing her.

Quickly, he ran a comb through his long, black, unruly hair. Its style fit his attitude these past six years. He was sure that before he started his new job, he'd have to get it cut and styled, for the straight and narrow business life he'd soon be leading.

He grabbed his phone without looking at it and then his bike. It was a Pinarello Gan S Ultegra weighing in at only 17.7 lbs. - it had been a birthday present from his parents. Around campus it was faster than driving a car and even on the road, he often passed them. Its only drawback was that there was no place for Lexi to sit; she had to ride her own bike. As he rounded the corner, he saw her parking her bike and going into the restaurant – he felt his heart skip a beat – she was beautiful beyond words and he loved her more than anything. He quickly parked his bike next to hers in the bike rack and entered the restaurant.

*　　　　*　　　　*

Lexi McDonald was born the only child of a Scotch Irish couple. Her mother, Heather, was highland Irish and her dad, Ros, fanatically Scottish and, as such, the house was never quiet for long. They always claimed that was why they only had one child – "too much shouting and cussing to make much love," her mother often said. Where Lexi was spirited, Alex was conservative – he had a calming affect on her and she filled him with life. She had had a conservative upbringing, raised Catholic. Her dad had worked in a shoe factory. Their life had been hard at first, but improved as her dad had been slowly promoted up the management ladder until making branch manager, enabling them to send Lexi to college.

They were looking forward to this special evening together to celebrate their graduations.

*   *   *

Two messages, from Alex's dad, had now accumulated on his phone and the last was much more urgent than the first. Alex's dad, the honorable Judge James Thornton was a self-made man – having come from a poor immigrant family having seven kids. Being the oldest, he'd worked to help support the family. His first job had been delivering newspapers – after picking up several routes, he hired some friends to work for him and took on even more routes until, at 17, he was made manager over all the paper routes. He'd lied about his age to get the job – they thought he was 22, the youngest ever hired for the position.

He'd been tough; he had to be to keep all his boys honest and serious about their jobs. A few had to be reminded of their responsibilities and he had the scars on his knuckles to prove it. Even with having to work, he was still able to graduate high school with honors. Every spare moment had been spent studying; he knew it was the key to "amounting to something", something that his dad always stressed or he'd end up working his whole life in the city sewers like his grandfather had. So, he got a few scholarships and went to college – compared to what he'd been doing, this was a cinch. When the other boys were partying, he was studying - he didn't have time for any of it. In no time, he'd made the Dean's list - which got him noticed, and more money to get by on as well.

He got his BA in less than three years and his Masters in Law by the time he was 22, a record for the college. He had taken the test for the Bar and had passed the first time up. He was the youngest to have ever passed the bar in the state of Massachusetts and was hired by a prestigious firm in Boston.

After working there for five years, he decided it was time to get out of the city – he'd met a nice girl from Iowa at college, and decided to move away from Boston to the less hurried life style of Des Moines. Once there, the easy going way of life and the people, pleased his nature. It wasn't long before they had Alex. He was the light of their lives and they spoiled him rotten. But, as Alex matured into a teenager, his father impressed upon him the seriousness of life and those lessons took. By this time, James was a District Judge and more recently appointed to a Federal judgeship – a very distinct honor.

Most recently, he discovered that Alex had taken a job that would keep him in Boston after graduating from Harvard. They had hoped that Alex would come home. and practice law as James had all these many years. However, they knew the pull of Lexi, who they had not as yet met, had a lot to do with his staying in Boston. They were looking forward to meeting her at graduation.

James had requested, and received, a copy of the paperwork regarding the new job his son had accepted with AgGIO Corps. After reviewing the paperwork and investigating the company, he concluded that his son had made a deadly mistake.

He had contacted the local FBI. After checking their records, they concluded it was a shell company connected to hundreds of others funneling their ill-gotten income to various accounts in the Caymans. He was almost afraid to ask where their income was coming from – but he did anyway ... he had to know.

The agent said, "As far as they could tell, it seemed to be coming from insurance companies."

"How is that possible?" James could feel his throat constricting.

"We are seeing a huge influx of money from an insurance company called "The Rock" in Boston. However, this new kind of crime was first detected out of their offices in the Triple Cities area of Broome County, NY, consisting of Centerville, Pleasantville and Hill Valley. There have been several deaths of insured's as "Key Men" to their respective companies with over a million dollars coverage. Since it is a common carrier accidental death, the insurance pays three times the face value, to the company for which the insured is employed.

"What can be done to prevent the insured from being killed?" James was barely able to ask.

"Well, I'd say to have him or her stay away from being transported or being hit by any type of "common carrier"; such as a car, truck, plane or any other type of motorized conveyance. As any insurance policies containing the accidental death, with the triple Indemnity rider - by contract has to payout out three times the face value of the policy. However, in this case since the policy is a property of a company and the company goes bankrupt, etc., the insurance policy could still end up being the property of whoever should buy up its assets and so it would continue until such time that the policy would be canceled for lack of payment.

He scarcely heard them say, "We are building a database of everyone who has been hired and insured by these shell companies, so we can not only build a case, but to warn them and provide protection".

He could hear himself mouthing his son's name, address and phone number and said he'd FAX the rest of the information to him. He pulled the file his son had sent and relayed the phone number to the FBI and then FAXed the information.

His hands were visibly shaking, as he hung up – he had to get in touch with his son before it was too late.

Again, he hit the recall button and heard his phone connecting and his son's phone ringing ... *"Please God, answer your phone, son...."*

*   *   *

It was 1 pm, the agreed upon time for the meeting between Chief Myerson and Samuel Ohonahee, the Regional Director of the FBI in Centerville.

Samuel had arrived early at Sharky's and had picked a seat in the back – the last one in the corner where he could see anyone coming or going from the front and back doors. He automatically took in everyone who was there, and mentally profiled them.

He knew this was one of the local watering holes - in fact the most popular in this part of the city. It'd been handed down from generation to generation and everyone knew who the regulars were. He immediately caught the eye of the bartender when entering and then the waitress. He heard the waitress's feet behind him pause as she picked up a menu and then continued to follow him to his seat.

"Are you expecting anyone else?" she asked as she sized him up.

"Yes, one other," he answered, nodding his head.

He heard the door open and saw that the Chief had arrived – there was a sudden hush within the area, as if, everyone was holding their breath. He silently wondered how many illegal's would be running out the back door.

"The bartender and two waitresses, recognizing him, said, "Hi Chief" as the Chief spotted him in the back.

Once seated, the waitress came back and asked what they'd like to drink and to let her know when they were ready to order. Both ordered ice water.

"I hear that the clams are to die for," the Chief said, as they looked at their menus.

"Yes, and the dishwashers have all run out the back door," Sam said nonchalantly.

"Yep, probably looking for some fresh clams," I suspect, the Chief said dryly.

"So, what's up, Chief – got a busy day going for me – how about you?"

"About the same," replied the Chief, unhurriedly.

"I hear you been running around in circles and finding dead ends," Sam said trying to find one of the Chief's buttons to push.

"Yeah, you heard right, that's to save you all that time."

There was a long pause as they debated which of the several entrées to order.

After the waitress returned and took their orders, the Chief cleared his throat. "I have reason to believe that one of my Detectives may be involved with the syndicate – you know, the one involved in these killings for insurance money. I have turned him into Internal Affairs to be checked out. He is an old friend; like family, and he explained the connection. So if, in your research, you should come in contact with him, please let me know – he isn't a bad guy, but he has had some tough breaks recently that may have pushed him over the edge. I don't know all the details yet, but as soon as I do, I'll keep you in the loop as I would expect the same professional courtesy. I'd rather you arrest him than for me to have to do it.

"What is the name of this Detective, Chief?"

"His name is Harold Scoville."

Samuel nodded his head, as if deep in thought, and then he said in measured words, "I'll see what I can do."

They finished their meal in near silence, punctuated with small talk about the restaurant and other good eating-places around town. Once finished, they both got up and the Chief picked up the bill, arguing that it had been he who had invited Samuel and it was only right that he paid the bill. They shook hands and parted.

*　　　*　　　*

Ryker and Katie had settled back into their usual routine. It had been several days since the FBI caught the man who'd shot at them and, as usual, outside of what they already knew, nothing more was gained. The FBI had set up taps on all known phone numbers, retrieved all past phone conversations and had made waveforms of the voices for future identification. They had also gone back in time using footage from thousands of cams known as CCTVs[15]. to track the "recruiter", but no ID had been established yet. This guy was smart – very smart - but, they knew sooner or later, he'd slipup and they'd catch him. Whether he would lead them to "Mr. Big" was hard to tell. One thing for sure, was that whoever had designed this organization, had used a process known as "phone modularization", most generally used by terrorists and spies. Each cell

---

[15] CCTV = Close circuit TV, monitored collectively with the use of special real time software.

was independent of the other, so no one knew from cell to cell to the next who, what or where each other was. Thus, they could never be compromised. However, in this case, it appeared that the modularization was even more finite. This model had been created with only one person per cell. No one seemed to know outside of their cell, who gave the commands or, who was in another cell working within their specialty. Other than the recruiter, whom they never saw again, there had been no face-to-face contact with anyone else. Now, even more alarming, the last people they'd caught had never seen the recruiter – they had been blackmailed by way of the contents of an envelope, which a courier delivered unwittingly from an unknown entity, as he was always paid with cash. All business was done by way of "drops", and commands received via burner phones, making it extremely difficult, if not impossible to connect the dots. What they needed now, more than anything, was a break; otherwise, many more people were going to die, because this model was being exported all over the country ... and beyond.

The old saying was, "follow the money". When they subpoenaed all the Cayman banks and filtered for accounts receiving deposits of over a million dollars, there were thousands. They were surprised by how many depositors were local US banks. They found several companies in operation and swooped in, catching people answering phones and doing other menial tasks, completely oblivious to the fact they were working for a shell company. Further, that their jobs would soon end, and along with it, the promise of future promotions. Again, their only contact with their manager was through the phone, whose number kept changing. This he'd explained was due to changes being made in their phone system – "it still had some bugs to be worked out," he'd gone on to explain.

If the FBI didn't get a handle on this, and quick, the murders of innocent citizens would become pandemic.

Katie, was glad that things were back to normal – even so, the FBI still maintained and worked out of the little house next door. She knew that her husband was still meeting with them, but would not tell her anything, except to say that they were no longer people of interest to the "bad guys". He had explained to her that since he was an Analyst, that he was bound by the Security Clearance guidelines and couldn't talk about FBI business.

Between this, his work at selling insurance, and now, discovering a new form of pension plans, he was finding little time for his family. And, worst of all, he was too tired for any form of intimacy – something she missed.

*　　　　*　　　　*

Now that things were back on track and the Abrams brothers were selling million-dollar polices again, Pete's next quarter's override was looking very promising. He felt like splurging by taking his beautiful wife to the Caribbean for a week - but, he knew he really needed to stay home – particularly since things could go sideways in a minute if he didn't keep his finger on the details. With all that he had going on, a week could be a lifetime – a lot could happen and he couldn't afford to lose control, just when the business was growing exponentially.

*　　　　*　　　　*

Thorn had been out of the office a lot and was counting on his new replacement for Susan - Peggy, who'd worked with Susan on many occasions, to pick up the slack. In Peggy's past position, they'd hired Florence, a young and attractive woman who caught his eye. If only he was younger, he would have taken her up on her obvious advances. But, for now, he had other irons in the fire that needed tending. The rapid expanse of his new enterprise was keeping him away from the office even more now than he'd expected. *If everything worked out, he'd be leaving this dump and making some real money.*

*   *   *

The Abrams brothers were again selling Key Man and Partnership insurance, though they were trying to qualify their clients better. They had to be people they knew, people within their families and the businesses to which the proceeds would be paid, were older businesses with well-established credentials.

In this pursuit, they had been asking about anything a family member might have noticed regarding "outsiders" asking questions about the family, or particularly them. Someone was trying to infiltrate their businesses for ill gain. Each family member they had talked with, agreed to help them, after all, that is what family is all about. Each gave it a lot of thought – *some remembered something, but nothing panned out - at least not yet.*

*   *   *

The FBI had arranged for Harold Scoville to come into their office in downtown Centerville. It sounded important, at least Harold had made it seem that way. It was also very unusual for a city detective to ask for a private meeting, particularly citing a "life or death" situation. Usually all meetings were arranged through their department leader, Chief Myerson. They quickly ran a check on the man and came up with a mixed bag of misery: a man not at the top of his game; just barely passing the test for Detective, marriage on the rocks, in hock up to his eyeballs and drinking heavily.

They were all seriously wondering what he could possibly offer them that they didn't already know.

At exactly, 5 pm, he arrived, somewhat disheveled and badly in need of a bath, shave and change of clothes. He introduced himself, as he shook Sam's and Vincent's hands. They immediately ushered him into one of their interrogation rooms.

"Okay, you called us – something about a *life or death* situation. What have you got for us?"

Briefly, Harold ran through his recent life's story, most of which they already knew, but when he got to the part where he'd been recruited by the syndicate, and then tossed a folder on the table, he got their attention.

The way he was recruited was not original - they'd seen it before and had even used it to "turn someone" to work for them. It was an old spy trick. With his recent history, it was no wonder they'd latched onto him to spy for them, he was a "candidate ripe for the picking".

Well, I gotta ask you – "are you willing to work undercover for us – which means that you will go on feeding information to the syndicate and us and doing business as always with the home town boys? If you do, we'll call off the bloodhounds and you get to keep your job. The private part of your life, you'll have to sort out for yourself ... have we got a deal"?

"Yes, we do," Harold, said as he nodded his head. Sam was thinking, *"now I have two informants inside the police force – what is this world coming to?* "Well, we better call Chief Myerson and tell him your working deep cover for us and to call off Internal Affairs, we don't need them getting in our way."

"Okay, now down to business, how do you get in touch with the syndicate?"

"I don't, they call me or send a message via currier," Harold replied.

"Okay, here's what I want you to do – as soon as they contact you, you call us using a public phone so you can't be traced and, needless to say, watch your ass that someone isn't watching you. We don't want to be shoveling you up off some road, just when we're becoming such good buddies." With a slight smile, Harold nodded his head - he knew the drill.

"What we need is to have time to triangulate and find where the other call is coming from and identify who's making it – getting us one step closer to whose running this organization." Sam knew that it was morphing by the day – spreading to other communities across the country, but, *so far,* it all had only one head that was controlling it. *God help us if some nefarious person or criminal organization discovers this "model" and decides to go into business for themselves.*

*　　　*　　　*

For the first time in weeks, Harold took a deep breath. The load on his back seemed to have fallen away. Just maybe, he'd be able to walk away from this mess, and put the rest of his life back together - after this was all over.

They'd seen him to the door and were glad for a break in the case – did they know more than they did before? Yes. Would he be useful to them? Yes. Sam felt they had gained some ground, but it would be a wait, and see, situation, the same as it was with their other operatives. Sooner or later, one of them would "*get the call*" and the ball would start to roll.

*   *   *

It was dusk, street lights were coming on all over the Triple Cities, as the sensors fell into the shadows of the surrounding hills and tree lined streets. It had been a quiet day. A few of the club members had stopped in for a drink and a chat; small talk about city politics, some sports talk and world events, then they'd gone home to their families. He'd watched the good-looking woman come down the street, look both ways at the corner, then cross the street. With the warmer weather, she was wearing lighter clothes and had changed her hairstyle – it made her look even prettier, if that was even possible. He fancied her, and he wondered how he might get to know her. Perhaps he would have one of his men build a profile on her. Yes, then he'd know how to or where he might just appear and strike up an acquaintance. Money could always bridge the age difference – and he had a ton of it.

The phone rang – even though the sound was muted, it always startled him, because he knew it meant the Boss was calling. That was the sum-total of what he knew about him, other than that, he could reach out at any moment and irrevocably eliminate him without even lifting a finger. No one would ever suspect who or what had happened – he'd just be another asset added to their already voluminous bottom line. He knew that as long as they needed him, he would be safe. It was the rule of the jungle – *eat or be ate.*

The voice was always distinct and forceful – this time, his order was to eliminate all assets. This would set in motion, a succession of hits. These were men whose only job was to see that the people in their files were systematically eliminated. They would all be called from a new burner phone, whose list changed with each calling, as their phones would be activated systematically, and never used twice. The instructions were the same, where to report to pick up their orders and, in their instruction folder would be the profile(s), money and two new burner phones - one to call back on to report when the job was done and one to receive where to pick up their next orders. It was a simple loop, completely self-contained, affording maximum anonymity. Once the phone call was made, the course of action, once started, was unstoppable. As Ben Galvani made each call, he discarded the phone and picked up another – they were all precoded with certain letters, followed by several numbers that matched up to new phone numbers. The new phones always arrived by a professional courier service. The man had no idea from who, or where the boxes came from, just that it was mixed in with all the rest, all shapes and sizes that he delivered to people all over the city. Whoever sent it, had simply stopped off at any one of their thousands of offices, where it was weighed, stamped, paid for and shipped. It was not unusual for packages to be shipped with no return address, so it was not questioned, as the receiving agent wished their customer a good day and asked the next one in line, how he might help them.

Ben wondered why all the assets were being eliminated all at once – must be something big underway, he reasoned. He also knew that he would be seeing a huge increase in claims being paid into all his shell companies and that his people would be twice as busy opening up new ones in not only NY, but all the surrounding states as well – business was good and it was growing. They had successfully migrated their business model to every state in the union and, within each state, the models were multiplying. The models under his control were producing hundreds of millions of dollars. He could only imagine, that multiplying that by thousands upon thousands of other offices that they must be talking in billions if not trillions of dollars, all flowing to off shore accounts. He knew that the Centerville Men's Club was becoming very wealthy and his commission was making him a very rich man.

Now he had to make up dozens of envelopes with new orders, two burner phones and two thousand in cash and sticky taped labels with the numbers of lockers. To the envelope, he'd also write the locker number. The last of this process, he'd have to wait until he got there to establish which lockers were available. As soon as this was learned, he'd write the locker number on a note in the envelope and, put it's key from the locker into the envelope after putting the money in the locker, and tape it under one of the seats back far enough so no one else would accidently see it.

Unbeknownst to him, his actions were being watched. As soon as he left the building, another man started tailing him.

*   *   *

Chief Myerson, had just received a call from the head of the Centerville office of the FBI and had been informed that Harold Scoville had turned states evidence and was working uncover for them. He had mixed emotions about the whole situation, but, especially about Harold. Knowing him on a personal level, he was glad he'd found a back door out of his professional mess, but still, he was disappointed in him for what he had allowed his personal life to become. Yes, holding a family together in this kind of business was hard – but when family problems loom large, it's time to get professional help and most cops couldn't seem to be able to admit that they needed help, until it was too late. He knew that it takes a special kind of women to make a marriage work with a cop. But, in Harold's case, it appeared too late, to salvage his marriage and maybe even his life. Reluctantly, he made the call to Internal Affairs and called off the investigation. Harold was now officially out of their reach - at least for now.

Secretly, he hoped that he'd straighten out and regain his balance in life.

Chapter 9.0

Benny Barstow had been under a Mack truck, changing the oil, when the burner phone rang. This was it; the moment of truth, he had to stall the caller without raising an alarm. He knew the Feds would be listening to his conversation and trying to locate the caller's signal source.

As before, the caller started immediately rattling off the directions ... "wait a minute, I can't hear you," Benny yelled as he started banging on the truck's frame with a hammer holding the phone close to where he was hammering.

"What's that you said?" He yelled.

Again, the man repeated himself as Benny continued to beat the hell out of the frame.

"Look, man, I got to get away from this noise so I can hear you ... there was a momentary silence on the other end, then a sigh, "OKAY ... but make it quick!" the man yelled back.

He was buying the Fed's some much-needed time and it was working.

Benny slowly counted to ten, and then said, "Boss, got to take this outside, okay?" He said it loud enough for the man on the phone to hear.

Then he waited another slow ten-count and said without yelling, "Okay, I'm outside – go ahead".

He could tell that the man on the other end of the call was pissed.

"You better damn well be," he said as he rattled off his new pickup directions and then he was gone. Again, it was the bus station and a seat number.

Benny's other phone rang, and a voice said, "Nicely done, Benny. We'll be picking you up at 12:00 pm, sharp at the usual place" and then he was gone.

*   *   *

Sam and Vincent were ecstatic and everyone in the war room was celebrating - finally a break in the case, after so many dead ends. They had finally gotten a fix on the signal.

Immediately, the FBI technicians went to work, pouring over a large map of the Triple Cities, working to pinpoint the caller's location. Using a straight edge and the coordinates from the triangulation of several phone towers, the lines converged over a large home on Beethoven Street.

"Gotcha," Sam growled.

It was one of those century old homes that were listed on the historical society's places of honor. They were often open to the public at Christmas and other special times of the year for viewing.

Sam immediately ordered a run down on the house; floor plan, who owns it, how the house is being used and anything else they could find. In the meantime, he started mobilization his plan. The sooner they hit the house, the better, but he wanted to be sure that they'd crossed all their T's and dotted all the I's, he didn't want anyone to get away to spread the word that the FBI was on to them or to have them get off on a technicality.

Benny, with a FBI team to monitor the pickup, went to the bus station. An advanced FBI agent was already at the scene to provide cover for Benny should anything go sideways.

As usual, Benny entered the station, bought a paper, approached the preselected seat as if he was considering others, and then settled on one, where he sat down and started reading the paper, as he unobtrusively looked around. Satisfied that no one was watching him, he dropped a part of his paper. As it drifted toward the floor between his feet, he reached down under his seat, tore loose a small brown envelope and, at the same time, scooped up his paper. The motion had been seamless. To the casual observer, nothing out of the ordinary seem to have happened.

After several minutes of reading the paper and observing his surroundings, Benny opened the envelope, which now lay, on his lap where no one could see it. Again, he found a numbered key. After a few moments, he gathered the paper, neatly folded it while walking over to the designated locker, opened the locker and withdrew a second, larger envelope. As usual, it contained two thousand dollars, along with the name and address of his next hit and their picture. It also contained two more burner phones.

From the first accident on, he had hated what they had him doing. He'd been tricked into the first one – which he had felt was an accident. But the evidence they had planted, made it look otherwise, then they had him push that car into a train and he knew that he was in too deep now to ever get out – they had him and it was now, literally, a case of do or die.

Sticking the money in his pocket, he gathered his paper around the envelope and exited the bus station, turned right and walked toward Main Street. He'd only gone a block, when a black suburban pulled up and stopped. The door opened, he got in and was whisked away.

Back at FBI headquarters, he was immediately taken to a holding room next door to the war room. Sam quickly joined them and shook his hand before sitting down.

"Okay, let's see what you got, Benny," Sam said.

Benny quickly tossed the envelope onto the table. Sam reached for it with a pen, and tossed it, pouring the contents out across the table. There was a momentary pause as they all eyed what it had held, then Sam retorted.

"Okay, Benny, anti-up. I know everyone wants a payday, but this time, we need it for evidence."

"Hey, a guy has to make a living, doesn't he?" Grudgingly, Benny reached into his pocket, took the money out and tossed it on the table.

As before, the forensic people came in, took pictures and dusted for prints and would check for DNA in the glue on the envelope once they got it to the lab – they'd already sent someone to the bus station to check the key and the inside of the locker for prints. Also, the underside of the seat was checked for any latent prints – usually, they could be found on the tape.

Most people don't realize that in dispensing tape, many times a print and DNA is left behind on the sticky side. The same goes for rubber gloves and, more recently, cloth gloves. Both can retain DNA that can be used in a court of law in identifying the donor.

They also had the name of the next hit – the man didn't know it yet, but he was about to become the luckiest man in the world. His name was Dennis Goodwin and a team was on its way to bring him in.

Just as they were digesting this bit of news, word came in from the agent planted at the bus station. He had the man followed from the bus station, to a house on Beethoven St. It appeared that he lived there as he'd parked somewhere behind the house.

"Damn," Sam retorted, could it be?!

"Ask him the address," he shouted to the man in the other room.

They waited breathlessly ... then it came in – it was the same as the coordinates from the phone triangulation.

"Holy crap, we have confirmation that the house is tied into this case – but we got to wait for all the information to come in – these people are smart and if we don't have our dominos lined up, they'll walk right out of jail as if we never shut the door and we'll never catch them. So, keep building our case, right up to the moment we get the search warrants. We don't want to tip our hand by having even the smallest bit of information leaked. *Remember, we want "Mr. Big" whoever he is.*

*   *   *

Dennis Goodwin was a recent graduate from SUNY Centerville. He'd been approached just before graduation by a job recruiter for AgGIO Corps. He learned that the company's headquarters were in Boston and that they apparently had connections to some highly placed people in Washington - so it was well funded. Dennis had always had a desire to work in a field that was "earth conscience" and this company represented the epitome of his philosophy. With all the benefits they offered and their LEED[16] rating, he was excited about his future with them and, what he could do to help save the planet.

Dennis was surprised, and a little annoyed to hear the doorbell ring, especially since they had security at the desk to ward off uninvited guests. He had rented the downtown "University Loft" because it was located where all the action was away from campus life. In all cases, the desk was supposed to call to let him know that he had company. Apparently, someone had once again talked their way past the unsuspecting desk clerk. He'd have to have words with them - then he remembered that he was

---

[16] Leadership in Energy and Environmental Design

a short timer. In a week, he was out of there and within two weeks, he would be starting a new job ... so really, what did he care?!

Looking out the peephole, he saw a couple of men in trench coats. A multitude of scenarios immediately played out; they were salesman wanting to sell him insurance, police asking around about having dope in his apartment, which he didn't, or the CIA was coming to recruit him. No insurance salesperson would have gone to all the trouble to look him up to sell him insurance, police asking to search his apartment – not likely, since he didn't have any dope, nor ever had – he'd only had a smoke at a party a month ago.

"Who is it?" he asked abruptly.

"FBI – we want to ask you a couple of questions."

He hesitated several seconds ... *"What the hell would the FBI want to talk to him about"?*

"Look, it's for your own good – we need to talk to you - now!" One of the men shouted from the other side of the door.

Dennis thought the agent might crash through it at any minute, if he didn't open it, now.

"Okay, okay, I'm not sure you're who you say you are, so how about showing me you're IDs."

He had to admit, that was gutsy of him, even if he was from New York. He was aware of what could happen – it could be some crook out to mug him and steal his money, as little as there was, max out credit cards and whatever else he had of value, beyond his dirty clothes and an iPhone.

As he looked through the peephole, he saw the FBI IDs, and felt reasonably sure that they were who they said they were – so he unbolted the door and let them in – ready to jump back at a moment's notice and take cover, if necessary.

After they'd requested his driver's license, to be sure that he was who they were looking for, they proceeded to ask him several questions, one of which was, "Had he recently been recruited by AgGIO Corps to work for them".

This question startled him – "why yes," he acknowledged that, "yes, indeed, he'd just been recruited by them at a very healthy salary and with great benefits".

Then the FBI proceeded to tell him about his life expediency and that AgGIO Corps was a shell company who was cashing in on the misfortune of their recently hired executives. All of which were dying in vehicle-related accidents and that a contract was out on him. That he was living on borrowed time.

"You're joking ... right? This simply isn't happening – nothing like this has ever happened before. I live a dull, normal life, the life of a bookworm. Just look at me ... no, no, no, really look at me – what do you see – that's right ... no one. I am the invisible man, who finally gets a job that his mother can brag to the fat bags in church about, and your telling me that I'm a dead man walking?! This is beyond anything that I could have imagined or could have dreamed. Talk about anti-climactic – damn it all to hell and back. Why don't you just pack up and leave me here – compared to your news, I might as well be dead, at least I'll make the papers by being in the obituaries. I'll finally be somebody - even if I'm a dead somebody!"

"Sounds like someone is feeling sorry for himself," the older FBI agent said, as he took his handkerchief out. "Here, take this and have a good cry – in the meantime, your coming with us – it's for your own protection, I'm sure your mama is not going to want to see you in a casket."

"Yeah ... I guess your right – let's go," he said reluctantly. With his head down and shoulders sagging, he followed them out of his apartment, shutting the door. *Where was his life going after this? He didn't have the foggiest idea.*

*   *   *

Alex and Lexi had just exited the restaurant, got on their bikes and were peddling side by side as they headed back to Alex's apartment. They were laughing and talking excitedly, failing to notice that a work-type van had pulled out behind them and was following at a discrete distance.

It appeared to be a painter's van as it had splotches of various colored paint around the back doors, black bumper and there was a faded, partially painted-over sign on each side. Iron rails ran across the top, which were currently supporting an extension ladder. Nothing seemed unusual about it, until one looked at the driver. His eyes looked straight ahead, seemingly unseeing, or was it perhaps, uncaring. They were like two periods in a pallid looking face – perhaps too long without sunlight, because the man had just been released from jail after serving 20 to life for 2nd degree murder. He had been released after only 15, due to his "good behavior". He had found work waiting for him, as he was picked up by a couple of old friends, who had connections, and just like that, he was back to work.

The phone started vibrating in Alex's pocket, but he chose to ignore it, as he was not only peddling up a grade but, he and Lexi were discussing their ultimate quest, which was the upcoming meeting with his parents. But, before that could happen, he had something else planned for the night.

Lexi hearing the phone, asked, "hey, aren't you going to answer it – might be your new boss calling," referring to his new job, as she knew how excited he was about the prospects of working for such an advanced company and being one of its key people.

"Nope, if it's important, they'll leave a message – right now, you're more important to me than any old phone call."

"Oooh!, you're the man, knowing all the right things to say to turn a girl's head," Lexi swooned using a sweet, as sugar southern belle accent.

He only smiled, as his plans for the night were playing out in his mind. He had even gone so far as to select their evening wear, rented a limo, and had paid for reservations for supper and an evening cruise.

*   *   *

Judge James Thornton, for the first time in his life felt helpless – a man who determined justice on life or death matters and sealed the sentence with a bang of his gavel, was now shaking with fear. His wife, passing his office and seeing him weeping, rushed to his side, horrified that something terrible had happened. She had never seen him cry – not ever. She dreaded knowing why and feared for the worst.

*   *   *

The van had picked up speed and was closing the gap behind them. The driver was waiting for just the right moment, to pass and sideswipe Alex; he had no intention of injuring the girl.

They had been peddling hard up a grade – traffic was not too heavy, but would be picking up soon due to the rush hour. Since he was the stronger peddler, he was perhaps two bike lengths ahead of Lexi, when he suddenly decided to take a short cut and shouted out to her his intentions, just as he shot across her path and onto a dirt biking lane leading through the woods that he knew exited near his housing.

The driver of the van saw his chance, as Alex was slightly ahead of the girl, giving him room to nudge him into the guardrails and then enter their lane and speed on ahead, with Alex plowing into the cables, going over the embankment and colliding with one of the numerous trees. It would be a sure and quick death.

Lexi heard, then saw Alex cut across in front of her and, as she followed him, a truck swept into their lane just as Alex disappeared to her right. She was already entering the bike trail, as the truck sweep by, nearly striking her.

"Damn bastard," she yelled at the top of her lungs, at the driver. "Some people just can't wait to pass bikers, even if it kills the biker - where are the cops when you need one?" she shouted."

Alex hearing her came to an abrupt stop, followed by her pulling up beside him, still fuming.

"Did you see that asshole that almost ran over us?"

"Yes, if I hadn't pulled across in front of you, when I did, he would have hit me and possibly you, killing us both."

"Makes me sick to think about it – idiots!!" she yelled again.

As the van disappeared on down the road, the driver was cussing a blue streak – he'd missed and now he had to start all over, setting up another "accident".

"*Talk about freak'n luck, that kid has it in spades,*" he thought.

*   *   *

Ben Calvoni had recently learned that Ryker was working for the Feds and it pissed him off. He thought that the first message, would have gotten his attention. It apparently hadn't registered, so he'd hired an out-of-town professional and, as yet, hadn't received confirmation that the job was done. They had earlier tried to warn Ryker off by trying to run him off the road. It hadn't worked, so they'd been forced to send another, more forceful, message – one Ryker couldn't turn his back on. He sat for several minutes thinking if he should just wait for a few more days to hear something or break the rules and call Jerry Carsdale. He knew he had better do something and do it quick, as he just remembered that the boss would be calling at anytime, wanting an update on all the "projects". So, he picked up a burner and called Jerry Carsdale's coded number. It rang several times – then stopped and a message came on, telling him to check the number and dial again. He knew then that his asset had been compromised. Now he'd have to tap another man. He also remembered that he had not heard from, Harold, his inside man at the police department. Strange ... he recalled that they had an agreement where he was to call in at least once a week and, as he recalled, Harold had never missed making his call. He'd have to check into what was going on. Quickly, he put a call out to his contact with the Buffalo mob for a professional and gave them the information. "When I hear that the job has been done, you'll get the cash, same as before," he said, and then he hung up.

He had no sooner hung up on the burner, and tossed it in the can, than the private phone rang – it was the Boss and he knew that he was not going to be happy with what he had to tell him. *His hands started to shake as he reached for the phone.*

*   *   *

At FBI headquarters, the tap on the Beethoven property caught a call that just went out to a phone belonging to Jerry Carsdale, who was currently being held for the illegal possession of a firearm, attempted murder, assault with a deadly weapon with intent to kill, and the list went on for another page. Bail had been denied for Carsdale. Even after a deal had been offered, he still hadn't talked.

There was no doubt that a person, or persons, at that Centerville Men's Club were tied to not only the attempted assault on Ryker and family, but also numerous other hits throughout the county and perhaps beyond.

Their investigations had uncovered the owner of the Beethoven property and The Centerville Men's Club list of philanthropy. They had been able to obtain a list of its members - all millionaires, all highly respected, prominent business owners, and all holding board positions all over town. These were not men to be trifled with ... they had to be sure their evidence was rock solid, before they made a move.

*   *   *

Detective Jerome Natelli had been running down every lead they had on the murders of both Bill Malone and Susan Willis. No matter where he turned, it was a dead end and it didn't' help that Harold was a no-show these days. He used to be a good partner, but lately, he'd asked for some time off to settle some personal matters. They lacked the manpower and the sophisticated equipment to search for leads through the deep web and by-way of the phone systems that were available to the FBI. He couldn't name the number of times that he'd uncovered a lead, only to learn that the FBI had been there days before. Frankly, he was tired and fed up with working for a department that seemed to be following a Loral and Hardy script. *It was almost as if, the city counsel didn't want them to catch the "bad guys".*

*   *   *

The FBI had just heard through their wiretaps, that someone in the Centerville Men's Club had contacted the Buffalo syndicate, taking out a new contract on Ryker – now they wanted him dead. It appeared that they were getting rid of all their loose ends, as several other assets had been eliminated within the past 12-hours. Most of these, weren't even in their database.

They'd have to put a man with Ryker and his family for their protection. From here on in, he was going to have to wear a bulletproof vest full time – "no if's ands or buts". The hard part was going to be telling his wife that the syndicate had put a contract out on her husband.

Sam immediately ordered Cal Benson and Shelley Winters to personally watch the Massey family. This meant being with them 24/7.

The nightly news shouted that vehicular accidents were suddenly up dramatically across the Northeast. Of these, most were hit and run, with a few being semis hitting cars and then leaving the scene of the accident according to the DOT. The governor wanted to know why.

*   *   *

The phone rang in the Boston office of the FBI, at 201 Maple Street, Chelsea, MA, Director Special Agent Harold Straw, answered, "Yes, what can I do for you, Director Special Agent Bernie Sandburg. Quickly, Bernie explained the situation involving Judge James Thornton's son, Alex, in the "Triple Indemnity" case, File D4016201. Additional information from the Judge, by way of his son, is being fed into the case file as we speak. The subject is believed to be listed for an immediate contract hit and is believed to be somewhere near Harvard, perhaps in the company of one Lexi McDonald, girl friend. A description of both will follow. Action: take into protective custody ASAP.

Immediately, the "take into protective custody" information was on the wire to every FBI and Police unit within the Harvard University area. Within minutes, it had filtered down to the University Security units to be on the look out for following two students and their pictures immediately appeared on all their mobile screens.

*   *   *

Frank Forestall had just finished a very long day. He was proud of himself, having recruited another ten students to work for AgGIO Corps. He had vastly improved on the process that he had been originally trained to follow. Instead of recruiting students one at a time, he was arranging meetings with ten or more in an on-campus, conference room. It gave him a sort of third party influence with the candidates, as if his program was sanctioned by the university. In addition, he tuned his presentation with "power words", like highly successful, envy of the business world, a beacon of hope and so on - always playing on their need to feel that they were doing something important for the environment. Making them feel empowered was also a powerful aphrodisiac, in getting them to sign on the dotted line. Since he had started, he had signed over a hundred students and there seemed no end in sight – he was sure to win the reward. He felt that there was no end to what he could accomplish. He had already received a raise and a bonus with more to come, they told him.

Because of his success, they were calling on him to train other recruiters, who were going to be representing other companies. He could not believe how successful he'd become in such a short time.

The money he made allowed him to live a life style that was only a dream a few short months ago. He'd already made over a half million in just six months, lived in the best rental high rise in Boston, some 50-floors above the streets. He wore designer clothes and had several beautiful women at his beck and call.

The door attendant had addressed him upon arriving and had held the door open for him as the valet took his keys along with a healthy tip and parked his Lotus in the underground parking area, covering it with a special protective covering as Frank Forestall had requested.

He glanced at his mail, as he approached the elevator – most of it was advertisements and several thank you notes from past students. The harshness of the marble lobby was tastefully softened with the use of palms and other exotic plants that framed a water feature that was over two stories high. Its gentle sound was designed to cover any echoes from voices and to soothe jangled nerves.

Entering the mahogany paneled elevator, he pushed the gold-plated PH-button[17] and then

---

[17] Pent House

inserted his security pass card. The doors closed and the elevator immediately shot up the 50-floors in 9-seconds. It was without a doubt the best part of his day, second only to driving the Lotus. There was the sound of air charging the brakes as the elevator slowed and stopped – then the door opened, leading into a spacious, fern decorated lobby with a couple of overstuff chairs and a settee on each side of his door.

Again, he inserted his card and heard the locks releasing the door that opened into a spacious living area. At first, it appeared that one could walk out, unimpeded, onto the clouds over the St Charles River. He never tired of the view and it was a real lady-killer – they all loved it.

Quickly, he disrobed in his bedroom, showered, shaved and dressed for the evening – it was time to play. He had already arranged for one of his favorites. She was a natural blond and drop dead gorgeous. She worked in the theater and could sing and dance all night, though he had other plans for her tonight.

Usually, he'd have a car pick him up and then his date, but tonight he felt like doing the driving and told her that he'd be by at 8 pm, to pick her up out front of her apartment complex. She lived about 15-minutes from his place – just a short drive down the boulevard.

The air was cool and the stars were out – never so bright, he thought as he stepped out the door and onto the gas lit street. His car was waiting for him – he was never tired of driving it. He hit the turn signal, pulled out and worked his way up through the gears, listening to the engine as the RPMs went up and down like yo-yos on a red string. It was music to his ears and, in no time, he was pulling up in front of Erin's Building.

He could see her from nearly a block away – drop dead gorgeous and all his. He quickly exited the car and opened the passenger side door, helping her in, and then he shut the door. She smelled of fine French colon and her lips shone blood red in the moon light as he gently kissed them.

"Where to?" she asked, her voice soft and warm.

"Oh, a bit of a surprise, I hope you don't mind heights." He said laughingly.

"Ooooh, just a bit of a hint, nooo?" she teased as she ran her finger through his hair just above his collar. He knew that she knew, what turned him on and she was off to a good start.

In no time, they were pulling up to the "Top of the Hub" the Rock's Center's crown Jewel on top of the Rock Tower. A valet took his keys and handed him a ticket, as he opened the door for Erin. In no time, they were in the elevator heading to the top.

Erin gasped in delight at the view – saying, "I know I'm in heaven now – just look at the stars," she laughed.

They were immediately seated by a set of windows at a fine linen covered table. Erin was grinning irresistibly from ear to ear as she looked in wonder around her.

They decided to order; her, the Peppercorn Rubbed Duck Breast and him, the 16 Oz. Prime Bone-in Ribeye. From the wine list, he chose the Petit Syrah Blend, "Machete", Orin Swift Cellars, Napa Valley, 2014.

From time to time, they would get up and dance to the live jazz which provided an excellent backdrop to this most memberable evening.

As it neared midnight, he signaled for his tab, and paid it with a generous tip as they prepared to leave, but not before she led him to a far corner, where they stood in front of the window, and she kissed him, long and deeply. They embraced for several minutes, and then parted, smiling, as he said, "let's put a night cap on the evening, at my place."

She nodded, "yes ... that would be very nice." They left and were soon back in the Lotus racing through the gears on the way back to his place, when the light changed and he was forced to pull up behind a garbage truck. The smell was atrocious and, just as he was going to back up and pull around it, another truck pulled up behind their car.

He had no time to react, as he heard both trucks accelerating with the one ahead, backing up and the one behind him moving forward. Too late, he realized what was happening; the last thing he would ever hear was Erin screaming....

The news the following day, reported a terrible accident – a car had been crushed between two trucks while waiting at a stop light, both occupants had been killed. The bodies had not been identified. *The police would continue to investigate the hit and run accident.*

Chapter 10.0

Ryker arrived home, at the same time as Cal Benson and Shelley Winter's. They were just ahead of him, so they motioned for him to pass them and open the gate. They had heard about the electric fence and wanted no part of it. Once inside, Cal closed the gate and rejoined them in the yard.

"Frankly, I don't know how I'm going to tell Katie, that there's a contract out on me," he told Cal and Shelley – "any rules you know of on how to tell a wife about such a thing?"

Shelley said, "tell her slowly, answer any questions honestly, while offering her support. You know, she's been through a lot already, so just put your arms around her and tell her how much you love and appreciate her and how much you need her to be strong for you and your children.

Katie had been watching from the living room windows, when Ryker arrived with a second car just behind him. She'd seen enough black Suburban's to know that it was an official government vehicle and assumed that there were two FBI Special Agents with him. They all appeared to be very serious about whatever they were discussing and she had the feeling she was not going to like what it was.

Thunder had sensed Ryker's arrival and was excited to see him, even though it had only been a few hours since he'd left. Upon opening the door, he rushed out and circled the new arrivals. Taking his queue from Ryker, he judged them to be non-hostile so didn't growl at them. But, he did huff a few times as he took in their odor, which he'd never forget. In the past few months, he'd been rapidly building his inventory of various new odors.

Ryker introduced Cal and Shelley to his wife and children. Right away Katie and Shelley embraced, while Katie told her how grateful she was for Shelley's understanding after the shooting.

Then Ryker said, "Can I get you anything to drink?" Both politely declined, as they sat down.

Ryker cleared his throat, "Katie, I have just learned something from the FBI that we need to discuss with you – would you mind having a seat with us?"

She looked nervously at both Shelley and Cal, as if to ask, "Oh, my God, what now?"

He could tell by the look on her face that she was fearing the worst and was about to lose it. She was not far from wrong in her assessment of the situation.

"Honey, I've just learned, from the FBI, that there's a contract out on me."

"What do you mean, a contract out on you ... what'd you ever do to them that they'd want to kill you," she wailed. Her voice reached levels that he didn't know a human was capable of.

Remembering what Shelley had told him, he tried to comfort her, telling her how much he appreciated her and how he and the kids needed her to be strong, right now.

"When will this ever end – haven't we been tortured enough!?" she sobbed.

No one seemed to have the answer, as the question hung out there in thin air like the smell of burned bread in a toaster.

He continued, Shelley and Cal are going to stay with us until the FBI can nail this guy and the people who hired him.

"Yeah, that will be the day – they're just too smart to get caught – you said it yourself, that crime has evolved, everything is done electronically."

Cal, spoke up, saying, "Yes, your right, and so have the tools we use to catch them. All I can tell you Mrs. Massey, is that right now, we are very close to shutting their whole operation down."

"That's right," Shelley replied. "I know how hard this has been on you, I've put myself in your shoes, given all that has happened – but you and your children are safe – I guarantee it. Also, your husband is very smart and when he's not here with you, he will be with us. Remember, there are a lot more of us, than there are of them and they will have to go through us to get your husband.

Katie seemed to brighten up some, knowing their commitment to her, her husband, and their children. Even so, she was still slightly rocking forward and back, as she kept saying over and over, "Dear God, please help us."

*   *   *

Pete had been on the phone the past few weeknights, and had not spent much time with his wife. She didn't seem to mind as she'd been in her office typing on her old manual typewriter and using her computer a lot. With getting his side business up and running, going out nights with his agents to drum up business and minding their home, he pretty much had his hands full. He also knew that he was neglecting his wife and it was starting to show, as she no longer was sharing the highlights of her daily activities with him or fixing supper – a meal that they used to enjoy together after a grueling day. He also remembered that they used to go skinny dipping evenings in the pool just off their bedroom. "Damn it all to hell," he growled at himself, I've got to stop working so much in the evenings and take some time with my wife ... before I lose her.

Quickly, Pete pushed his chair back and got up from his desk. "There's no time like the present to get out of this rut," he thought to himself. He knew it wouldn't be long before he'd have all the money he ever needed to do anything in the world that they wanted, at any time. All he needed was just a few more weeks.

He opened the door to his office that he always kept closed so there would be no distractions while he was working. When the house was built, he had instructed that, not only the house be sound proofed, but especially his office. Further, that it would have no windows – only a skylight. The doors to his office were pocket doors; heavy as those on any vault, and lockable. The floor was hardwood, but covered with an oriental, handmade carpet, that accented his work area. The subtly lit murals on two of the walls provided a feeling of space, preventing any feelings of spatial deprivation. On the remaining walls were built-in mahogany, floor-to-ceiling bookcases that tied into the deep mahogany coffered ceilings. The bookcases served two purposes, one, the obvious to hold books, the second was not at all obvious and that was to provide a secret exit from the room. A narrow hallway from it, ran down some stairs where he could either access a special harden survival room, or he could go, under ground, beyond the pool and come up through an escape hatch in the pool house, that also doubled as a guest cottage, which they never used. It intrigued him to be able to leave his office without alerting his wife to his departure. *He had often used this feature to come and go.*

Leaving his office, he crossed the hall and knocked on her door, before opening it – but the knob didn't turn; it was locked. "*Curious,*" he thought. "*Why would she lock it?*"

She'd heard his knock, and hurriedly put away her work and rushing to the door, she apologetically said, "Oh, I must have accidently locked it, without thinking".

"Is there something that we need to talk about?" he gently asked her, his arms now around her, gently holding her close. "I know these past few weeks, I've not been here for you, especially, the ... evenings. I've been up against it with insurance problems. It seems that all those accidental deaths are bad for business. But the sales train is back on its tracks, again."

She nodded her head understandingly, as she said, "well, I sensed that you were having a problem that you were working through and I didn't want to pry, so I kept myself busy with my online blogging and Pinterest".

"What in the world is that?" his voice sounding mystified.

"Blogging is an online forum where you can expound upon something that your good at to help others or that may be of interest to your readership and Pinterest is an online website full of all sorts of clever ideas."

"Oh, sounds interesting – I bet you're very good at it, as I find you to be a very interesting woman ... and, I need to explore those interests even more – so how about we make this a date night?"

She could hear the passion in his voice – "*perfect,*" she thought, "*she'd been hard at work on her own little surprise, just for him ... and she needed a break.*"

They showered together and after a short, intimate detour, they were ready to go out. He had already booked a reservation for later and he'd even thought to rent a limo for the night. Nothing was too good for Amelia – tonight was her night and he intended to go all out to make up for his dereliction of duties and the appearance of taking her for granted these past few weeks.

He heard the buzzer sound, announcing that their car had arrived. He pushed the button on the intercom and asked, "Yes."

"Good evening Mr. Fordson, I'm here to pick you and your wife up, may I drive in?"

"Yes, you may," and he pushed the button allowing the gate to open.

"Just a minute, dear, I forgot something ... I'll be right back," she whispered in his ear as she rushed off back into the house.

True to her word, she was back, her eyes sparkling with anticipation of what this new adventure might bring.

Taking Amelia, by the arm, he escorted her to the door. He noticed that she was now carrying a slightly larger bag than before – there was no accounting for the taste woman had in their many varied clutches and bags.

Her hair shown like molten gold, as it trailed down over her lightly tanned shoulders and onto her pale blue evening dress. As she walked, her long legs played peek-a-boo with the world, as they momentarily left the confines of the dress through hidden slits in the short nearly transparent chiffon dress. Months of training and workouts had toned her body into a figure that even the Greek God Venus would have been envious.

On the way, they sipped Champagne and held hands, as he looked deep into her blue eyes – he had never loved anyone as much as he loved her. He silently vowed that he would never again, allow his work to get in the way of "there time together" – never again."

The driver announced, through the intercom, that they had arrived, as he pulled up to the entrance.

Immediately, he showed up at the door, opened it and stood by as Pete exited the limo, giving his wife a hand helping her out. The driver turned his face away as her dress slid far up her long slender legs. They were welcomed at the door by the maître de, who personally saw them to their table. Upon pulling out the chair for his wife and he was seated, the maître de, signaled to the Server to approach the table. Pete had told them, when calling for a reservation, to spare no expense – that this was to be something special for his wife.

Pete could tell by the look on his wife's face, that she was impressed as she smiled radiantly. Everyone's face had turned to watch as they'd entered the room and had been seated in a private sitting area off the main dining room.

A wine list had been presented, for them to make their selection. He ordered 97 Laurent-Perrier NV Grand Siècle Grande Cuvée Brut Champagne, after the wine connoisseur explained its history and stated that it was from the Laurent-Perrier US Cellar Selection, which he knew was quite exclusive.

After a toast to one another, and a couple of sips of their champagne, it was time to order - again, their server came and took their order, after detailing each selection. In no time, their food arrived. She was served Shrimp Marsala and he Steamboat Willie.

They engaged in small talk, as they sat side by side near the window. Seeing that she had started to shiver, he gallantly removed his coat and placed it around her shoulders. As he did, he caught the aroma of her perfume and remembered the many nights they had spent together. Her perfume that night was like a signal of things to come.

Again, taking her by the hand, he told her that he was sorry for the weeks of not being available to her and would she forgive him.

"Don't be silly, Pete, there's nothing to forgive – its okay, you have your job and I have my interests – so what is to be sorry for? I know that there will always be those times when you, or I, will get involved in something and then time flies by until we can refocus on each other again – it's to be expected."

Pete felt relieved that she didn't hold his absences against him – that was what he loved about her - her independence, her drive and ability to take hold of a project and see it through, no matter what.

He called for their check and she excused herself to go powder her nose, giving him a hug and kiss as she grabbed her bag and left the table. He retrieved his coat from the back of her chair where she'd left it, got his phone out and called the chauffer to bring the limo around.

The maitre de came by and asked if everything was okay, and Pete told him that everything was excellent and that they most certainly would be returning. The server came by and presented him with the bill, which he okayed and sent his credit card back with her.

He sat there for several moments, waiting for Amelia to reappear, hoping that she was okay. It was unusual for her to take this long. His thoughts were interrupted by the server as she returned with his card and voucher.

"I'm sorry sir, but your card was rejected for insufficient funds." She looked distraught for having to bring him this news.

"That's impossible," he heard himself say in as controlled a voice as he could muster, given the circumstances.

"Try it again, I know that there is enough in there to buy and sell this restaurant, twice over." In the back of his mind, he was becoming unsettled as to why his wife was taking so long – was she okay?

"Sir, I tried it several times and it keeps being rejected," the server persisted.

"Okay, okay, try this card," and he handed her his American Express. Surely this one, which he had never used, would work. He was feeling very annoyed, that his wife still had not made an appearance and that his credit card had bounced – *"What the hell was going on?!"* The bank would be getting a piece of his mind, come tomorrow morning. When he was done with them, they'd be lucky to have a job.

He was about to go back and kick the Lady's Room door down, when the server and the maitre de both appeared.

"Sir, we are extremely sorry, but your American Express Card has also failed to work, we have no other recourse, but to call the police about this matter."

"Look, I'll pay you in cash – I think I have enough in my wallet to easily cover the bill." Frantically, he reached and pulled his wallet out of his coat pocket, it felt strangely light, upon opening it, he saw only one dollar and he was also missing his driver's license and registration to his car.

"My God, what the hell is going on?" For the first time since he'd been a kid, his voice sounded weak, and very frightened.

Through the haze of his state of confusion, he was aware that a couple of security people were beside him. They were telling him to put his hands behind his back. He numbly obeyed and they hand-cuffed him.

He was glad that they were still in the private room and not out in the main dinning room, as he was sure there were people out there who would recognize him.

He had no idea what was going on or why, but he had one over-riding concern and that was for his wife, as he shouted, "my wife's missing, she hasn't come back from the Ladies Room yet. Will you please send someone to see if she's okay!?"

The maitre de signaled the server to go back and take a look. In the meantime, a couple of police officers walked in and Pete recognized them as the two who had interviewed him about the guy getting hit by a truck a few months back.

"Finally, someone who can help," he reasoned as he yelled out to them, "Jerome - Harold, we got a misunderstanding here and my wife is missing, can you help me?"

"Aaah, our favorite insurance man – I see you're on the other side of the spanking stick now – so who are you bilking out of their hard-earned money this fine evening, sir?"

After several minutes of trying to explain, what had happened and about his missing wife, he learned that she was not in the bathroom or anywhere else in the building.

They exited at the rear of the building, to spare Pete the embarrassment of being paraded through the dining room. Harold spoke to the limo driver who was told to bill Mr. Fordson for this evening's service and they would see that he was paid. Then Pete was taken a few blocks across town to the police station and put in one of their interrogation rooms, which, he was already familiar, and where he waited for his lawyer to show up.

He kept thinking that this was all a bad dream, a thought that was only interrupted by his desperate need for a cigarette.

Pete was in shock about his missing wife; frantic to know what had happened to her. How, and or why, would she be missing – it was just incomprehensible. All he could picture in his mind was her lying on the side of the road, injured or worse.

He was also upset about his charge cards being charged to the hilt. He couldn't think of any way in which they could have been compromised. In fact, most times, he had used cash – other than using his personal visa card to make the reservation for the limo, he'd not used them in weeks – in fact, he'd never used the American Express Card. He'd gotten it to use during their over seas vacation. They'd even gotten their Visas in preparation for the trip.

In the course of his questioning, his lawyer showed up and he was released.

Also, to expedite the process of finding his wife, he gave the police full access of his home, before he was allowed to return. His lawyer explained that the police needed to rule him out as a suspect – sometimes it turns out to be the spouse who is found to be guilty in such disappearances. He also asked him if there was anything of a "private matter" that he had not put away in a lock box or safe, before they would consent to allowing the police to have free access to his home. Pete couldn't think of anything that he might have left out, that would violate any of his clients in anyway. He was always very careful about such things.

*   *   *

Thorn Carbine had returned home from Boston and immediately went to his office. The girls in the office had hardly heard a word since his sudden departure and all were a twitter over what may have happened. Their stories ranged from being fired, to that of having more underwriting restrictions applied to their already mounting workload.

His first request was that all Sales Managers and the Office Manager report to him by 9am. Within the allotted time, they all came trooping into his office like attendees to a wake.

Once seated, he told them about his trip to Boston, how they had grilled him about every facet of their sales of Key Man and Partnership type insurances. They wanted to know how it was marketed; sales approach, qualifying interview, amount of sale and how it was arrived at, right down to the delivery of the policy. Then they set about making changes in the underwriting of these types of policies, the details of which would be forth coming in a week or so. Then he had excused them and after shutting the door, he'd collapsed in his 500-dollar manager's chair and lapsed into a long period of silence – *his mind escaping to his new life far away from this place.*

*   *   *

Alex and Lexi, had dressed for the evening, neither one of them in all their years of knowing each other had ever been dressed formally, and both were standing in front of the hallway mirror, taking in the spectacular change in one another.

"Gorgeous, he exclaimed" as his eyes locked onto her.

"What a hunk," she laughed, "brains, looks and brawn – who would have guessed," she exclaimed as she giggled.

The sound of a horn honking signaled that their ride was waiting. He, as yet, had not told her where they were heading – it was to be a surprise.

He had earlier, muted his phone, as he did not want it ringing and interrupting his plans for the night.

The limo threaded its way through the streets of Boston, until it finally pulled up to 200 Seaport Blvd. At the pier was tied The Spirit of Boston. Lexi gasped as she saw the ship and her eyes started to tear up. Their picture was taken as they stood on the gangway in front of the "Spirits Signage".

As he turned toward her, he could see tears running down her cheeks and her lips were trembling, as she said, "Do you know how wonderful you are? I love you more than anything."

He handed her his linen handkerchief to dab around her beautiful, limpid blue eyes, saying, "No, but I hope you'll keep reminding me everyday of our lives." To which she gave him a poke to the chest.

They continued up the gangway and boarded the ship. A server was waiting for them and, after looking at his tickets, she showed them to their reserved seats.

Lexi noticed that the seats were right near a railing, which was one level higher than the stage that was dead center below them. Apparently, there would be entertainment while they ate.

Hardly had Lexi taken in the well-decorated interior than their server inquired as to how they wanted their food prepared; his steak, medium rare and her lobster sautéed with garlic and butter. She wanted her broccoli with cheese sauce and he, a baked potato with butter and sour cream.

"Well, what do you think, sweetheart?" he asked her.

"Well done, my dear," she responded as her eyes were still taking it all in. She had never seen or been on a boat this size and was awed by everything she saw; the brass hardware shown like gold against the dark Mahogany woodwork and the overhead was a maze of carved, cove ceiling work.

She noticed that the boat had started to move and watched as the dock slid off from view to their stern. The movement was so slight that had she not been looking, she would never have noticed they were underway.

Every so often, the Captain would call their attention to a ship or a building as they passed it. She remembered his talking about "The Constitution" or "Old Ironsides", as she was lovingly referred to by those who served on her, back in the day.

Once the meal was finished, the servers all appeared on stage, minus their server uniforms and proceeded to entertain them. After several songs; some jazz, others contemporary, the Entertainment Director, took the mike and thanked all the singers for a wonderful performance. Then turning toward the audience, he said, I'd like for Mr. Alex Thornton and Miss. Lexi McDonald to come down here.

Lexi's mouth dropped open and her eyes got wide as she watched Alex stand up and reach for her hand. She was no singer – why, she couldn't even carry a tune, even if her life depended on it, but she followed him down the brass-edged stairs, while hanging on to the brass railings.

A couple of ushers helped her navigate the stairs to the stage, as Alex followed her. As they turned toward the audience, there was a stillness that she would never forget … so many faces, the lights and air of expectancy, were all washing over her. Then she looked at Alex as he took the mike. What was he going to do, sing to everyone, while she looked on? Then she saw him go down on one knee and, with his free hand, he was holding open a ring box. From it, he took the largest diamond ring she had ever seen, and holding it up to her, he asked, "Lexi, you are the girl of my dreams, my-everything; my sun, my forever girl, will you marry me?"

Her world started to spin as she felt her head nodding, "yes". He stood up and placed the ring on her finger, to the cheering of hundreds of people. He put his arm around her to steady her as he led her off the stage, the cheering still echoing throughout the ship.

Once again, in her seat back at their table, all she could do was to look at the ring and smile – it was no ordinary smile, it was the biggest, happiest smile she had ever made. She felt Alex's kisses upon her face, and her arms found him in an embrace that she never wanted to let end. The ring was a signal of his commitment to her – they'd been going together for over two-years and, in that time, she had gotten to know him as he had her, but they had never discussed the "M" word or having their own "family". She had wondered about meeting his family, feeling insecure, especially after being together for over two years and not a hint of any commitment on his part toward her – but now she felt secure in her position in the family as his fiancée.

*   *   *

Nearby, in the far side of the Spirit of Boston's parking lot, a large, four-wheel-drive truck with roll bars over the top and a bull bar guard over the front bumper, stood waiting, its high-performance engine rumbling. They had caught up to Alex again – this time, they wouldn't miss.

In the distance, he could see the lights of the ship returning to the dock. *The man at the wheel tightened his grip on the steering wheel, mentally rerunning his plans to get Alex. Only he was their target, but if his girl friend happened to get in the way ... oh, well, sometimes there's collateral damage that can't always be helped – shit happens.*

Chapter 11.0

J udge James Thornton, had tried one more time to get in touch with his son and had failed, now it was time to take action – if there was still time.

He'd reached out to a friend of his – also a Federal Judge - and had told him what he suspected, given the evidence that he'd dug up and now shared with him. Within minutes, his friend issued a "Protective Custody Order" and wired it, with the information Judge James Thornton had provided, to the FBI headquarters in Boston. They, in turn, checked their database and located both the "Boomerang File" and information on Alex Thornton; the Judge's son. They immediately issued a Top Priority" BOLO on Alex Thornton.

All over Boston, police, FBI and security units were receiving a picture of Alex Thornton and a coded, High Priority message indicating that he was in imminent danger. He was thought to be in the company of one Lexi McDonald – girlfriend. Even cab drivers with two-way radios were getting the message.

The limo driver was a part time EMT and he'd heard the alert come over his two-way radio and immediately knew that it was his clients that they were looking for. He answered the call, giving his GPS location. It was confirmed and he was told to hold his position - they were on their way.

In the distance, from several points, he suddenly heard sirens piercing the darkness.

The message had also reached The Spirit of Boston and the radioman informed the Captain of the situation. He got hold of the Master at Arms, who gathered a couple of his Security Detail and headed for Alex Thornton's table.

*   *   *

Alex and Lexi decided to cap off the evening by going above decks to enjoy the openness of the sea, as the ship made her way back to port. Here and there, well-wishers congratulated them, wishing them a long life together.

He ordered a bottle of their best Champagne on ice and it was brought to their table as they gazed over the rail at the harbor lights and the stars above. Suddenly a shooting star lit up the sky and they made a wish on it, laughing as each tried to guess what the other had wished for.

In the distance, above the swish of the sea against the sides of the ship, and the gentle murmur of voices around them, they heard several sirens.

"Talk about New York, the city that never sleeps, I think they should include Boston in that appraisal," Alex, said.

She only nodded, as she said, "I hope whatever or whoever it is, that it's nothing serious – not on our night ... or any other time - really, why can't there be more happiness in people's lives, you know, the kind of happiness that we have, right here, right now?!" Then she smiled that smile at him again. It was the one that lit up his world and made him believe that he was the luckiest man in the world.

He nodded, and smiled slightly, because he understood her mood – he felt it as she did; their love for one another and the joy it was bring them.

It seemed as if all the people on board were swarming around them, watching over the rail as the ship neared shore. He poured another glass for each of them and taking her by the arm, they too, leaned up against the railing and he toasted her. "To a long and happy life, my love, may we never grow too old to love and care about each other ... in life and in death."

*   *   *

Security was scrambling all over the Spirit of Boston, looking for "the couple" but they'd seemed to have disappeared. Then a check of their orders showed that they had just ordered Champagne and it was coded to a table on the observation deck near the Starboard railing. But, by the time security got there, they had mixed in with the crowd as it moved toward the exits.

The FBI having heard the location, sent in by a limo driver, thought, "What a break," as they transmitted their tactical plan, as several of their cars were rushing toward the piers. Upon entering the parking lot, one of the cars hung back to watch for any suspicious activity, while the others rushed toward the pier, positioning themselves for a quick exit.

The parking lot was full of tourist's cars, some with people in them waiting for loved ones to disembark, and others empty.

Their agents, along with the police, flooded the area, all waiting and looking for anything that seemed out of place. They knew that the assassin could be anywhere, but most likely, in a large truck per their usual MO. They had been fully briefed about the information in the "Boomerang File" and the method used to kill their victims.

Two large refrigerated trucks were spotted near the pier, which turned out to be food delivery trucks for the ship. They were there for a pickup and to deliver the following days supplies. The driver's checked out and their invoices were all in order.

The ship had arrived on time and shortly, the passengers started disembarking from two exits - one near the front of the ship and the other near the stern. Quickly, the police and FBI put people at each point, to watch for Alex and Lexi without being obvious. From time to time, they would glance at the pictures on their iPhones and compare them with the people walking toward them.

On the far side of the parking lot in an elevated 4 x 4-turbo super-charger truck, the man behind the wheel noticed the increase in activity near the pier. Looking closely, he could see that several people around the pier appeared to be plain clothed cops. He reasoned that they were there to apprehend some criminal that was coming off the boat. It didn't occur to him that they were there to pick up the person he'd been ordered to "take out".

Arm in arm, Alex and Lexi left the ship walking down the gangway, when suddenly, two men in trench coats grabbed hold of them.

"Alex, we're FBI, sent to put you both into protective custody," one of the men said as he flashed his badge. Alex watched as two more agents fell in ahead of them and two behind.

"Protective custody, what the hell are you talking about?"

"It's been ordered by a Federal Judge out of Iowa – there is a death contract out on you," replied the agent beside him, who apparently headed this operation.

They were quickly ushered into the back of a big black suburban that was equally as black inside. "Apparently, the courtesy lights weren't working," Alex reasoned.

"What about my driver waiting for me back there in the limo?" Alex asked.

"We'll take care of him," the man beside him assured him.

A police officer at the scene, heard the conversation on his radio, saw the limo, and told the driver to send the bill to his client as he'd taken another way home. "Limo driver taken care of," he reported, as he released the button.

As the Suburban approached the parking lot exit, they caught a blur from the side of the car as something was coming toward them at a very high speed. Before they could react, it broadsided the car.

The impact was so violent, that the Suburban wish-boned, and then, from the inertia, rolled over, and burst into flames.

The vehicle hitting them became airborne, landed on their rolling car, rolled over onto its wheels and drove off, disappearing into the darkness.

One of the police cars took chase, as the others rushed for emergency equipment to help free the occupants. An APB was sent out on the fleeing vehicle and now others were joining in the chase.

Inside, everyone was stunned. Alex, reached for Lexi, but couldn't get a rise from her. The driver was feverously trying to kick out the windshield. From outside, men were pulling on the doors and trying to kick in the glass. Finally, with the use of a crowbar, one of the doors was forced open and those who could, scrambled to safety while dragging the others near them outside the car.

Carefully, as the fire was now venting through the Suburban, Alex and another officer, worked to extract Lexi. She was unconscious and covered in blood.

Alex was beside himself, as he knelt beside her, his clothes still smoking from the fire. His only care was for Lexi, who was laying there so quiet on the cold hard pavement. One of the police officers took her pulse and started CPR. The EMTs arrived and one took over, while another inserted a breathing tube and attached it to an oxygen supply.

"We've got to transport her now, if we have any chance of saving her", the medic yelled. Several hands reached to support her as they put her carefully on a gurney and into the ambulance. Following close behind, were Alex and two FBI Agents.

As they sat in the ambulance, the Medic's worked feverishly to save her life – with sirens blaring, the ambulance sped to the nearest trauma center.

"Who and why would anyone want to kill me?" he asked though his tears.

"It's part of a syndicate operation to kill people for the insurance money." He explained briefly.

"Damn, dad was right about AgGIO Corps. If only I'd listened, this wouldn't have happened," he said, as he gestured wildly at nothing in particular with his hand.

"It's because of your dad's action, that you're alive to talk about it now."

He knew his father was a man of action, so this was not surprising to him – if only he had taken the time to answer his damn phone, this would not have happened – it was all his fault.

"You know, I just proposed to Lexi tonight on the ship – we were so happy – now look what's happened," he choked, and with his hand over his face, he started to sob.

Suddenly, the ambulance stopped, the oxygen was turned off, the paddles were applied and a shock delivered causing Lexi to arch and drop back onto the gurney. They all watched as twice more, they applied the paddles and again, she arched, before the EMT reported a sinus rhythm.

Again, they were in motion, arriving within minutes at the EMERGENCY ROOM ambulance entrance. Several attendees, who had been waiting their arrival, rushed out to meet them, with medical information being exchanged as they ran along side the gurney into the Intensive Care Unit. To anyone not familiar with the routine, they would have thought it was chaos, but, in reality, it was a highly organized effort to save lives.

Alex and the two FBI Special Agents were led to a room off the ER, where they waited to hear any updates on Lexi's condition.

Several hours ticked by, and as they waited – Alex slowly told them from the beginning how he'd been hired by AgGIO Corps, about his dad being skeptical of them, right up to his purposing to Lexi.

He realized now that the near accident between him and a truck while biking home a few days ago, was not just a happen stance, but an attempt on his life, that had failed. Now they had tried again and, because of it, Lexi had been seriously injured.

Unconsciously, he looked at his phone and noticed all the messages from his dad; some text and others voice. After looking at the text and listening to the voice mail messages, particularly the last one, he was filled with remorse … if only, he had paid attention, perhaps none of this would have happened.

They heard a sound outside and then the door flew open and his parents rushed in. He had never been so glad to see them. After embracing, the Agents introduced themselves and, his parents were updated on what had happened so far.

Alex's mother said, "We should pray – she's going to need all the help she can get".

This was a side of his mother that he had never seen, but welcomed, given the situation. So, they prayed, asking God for His intercession, that he make Lexi whole again. It was not that long a prayer, but it was heartfelt.

Most of the time, there were long silences, as the minutes, then the hours, ticked by while they searched their souls to gain a deeper understanding of what the value of life really means.

*　　　*　　　*

Chief Bill Myerson had called in his two best detectives, Jerome and Harold to go over to Pete Fortson's home and have a quick look around. They were to look for any evidence concerning Pete Fordson's missing wife. He had gotten permission from Pete to search his house for anything that might lead to them locating his wife. At the moment, he was downtown with his lawyer.

Upon finding the house, they quickly noted that it had enough security to double for The White House. They checked back with the Chief for the password so that they could enter the grounds and if there were another for the house, if so, they'd need that one too. While they waited to hear back, they started looking around. The home was set on an unusually large lot, several acres, Jerome guessed, most of it wooded, which kept the house from being seen from the road. A stone and cemented post, with heavy iron fencing between each upright ran around the perimeter. It was easily over 10 feet high, he estimated. To build something like this, had to have cost a fortune, Jerome thought.

The security code came to them via a text message, along with a second code for the house.

Getting back in the car, Jerome punched in the code and the huge iron gate parted, reeling back out of sight into the stone entranceway. The drive was made up of cobblestones like those seen leading up to the old Mansions found back in the hills of merry old England. It wound zigzagging up around the floral landscaped hill and ended in a sort of courtyard in front of what appeared to be a small mansion. They both whistled at the sight.

"Hmmm, off hand, I'd say this man's credit cards wouldn't bounce – something isn't right about this picture," Jerome whispered under his breath, as if afraid someone might be listening to their conversation.

After getting out of the car, they approached the twin doors, punched in another code and when they heard a buzzing sound, they pulled down on the heavy brass handle which caused the door to unlatch. Using his shoulder, he pushed the massive door open and entered what looked like a gallery. Its floor was made up of polished cobblestone very much like those in the driveway. Everywhere they looked, they saw opulence unlike nothing they'd ever seen before. It was built on a scale that resembled the Biltmore in North Carolina. He remembered having seen it once, when he and his bride had visited the area on their honeymoon.

Taking turns, they worked their way through the whole home. Repeatedly, they'd look at each other and shook their heads – definitely, this guy had some money. However, neither one of them saw any signs of foul play involving his wife.

Finally, they were at what appeared to be Pete's and Amelia's offices – they checked her file cabinet, desk files, under the blotter, in the drawers and found nothing out of the ordinary. Next, they checked his office. At first it appeared to be okay – again, no evidence of him doing his wife in, or what may have happened to her, until they looked in the far back side of his top center, desk drawer and found a file folder. It had been their experience that most people, when they had something to hide, hid it there, thinking that surely, no one would ever bother to look there. But, through training and years of experience, he never failed to check and was amazed at how often he succeeded in finding what he was looking for.

At first, the contents in the folder looked like a ledger; names of people and, after that, million-dollar figures, then a column showing that number tripled, followed by the cost of doing business and net profit columns. On another sheet appeared a list of banks, followed by account numbers.

Slowly, Jerome's hair started to stand up, and then he showed it to Harold. At first, Harold only shrugged his shoulders as he started to dismiss it - then he said, "Holy shit – I think we've found "the Boss"".

Quickly, they radioed the Chief and told him what they'd found – "Frankly, Chief, we need someone over here that knows this man and his wife – hate to say it, but we need the FBI and that insurance guy – Ryker, in on this – they know a lot more about this case than we do."

"Your right," he heard the Chief say grudgingly – and we don't want to muddy the waters – what you've found can make or break us. I'll make the call, stand-down, don't touch anything, and don't let anyone in but the Feds, they'll be coming your way in a few minutes, and the phone went dead.

"Well, what do you know – so this guy, that we we're holding, is the Boss of Boomerang," the Chief thought to himself. He also liked the idea, of Samuel Ohonahee owing him for a change. Smiling from ear to ear, he made the call.

After hanging up, he made the call to the DA to have a warrant for the arrest of one Pete Fordson for murder and fraud and a search warrant for Pete's house making anything that they found admissible as evidence for a trial.

*   *   *

Ryker heard Sam's usual gravely voice, say, "Yeah, Chief, what can I do for you?"

Sam was wondering what the Chief wanted now. After a few minutes of listening, Sam said, "Vincent and I will be right over, along with Ryker, and he dropped the phone.

"Seems the Chief and his men found a hidden file in Pete's desk in his home, that provides the evidence that he's the head of the syndicate," Sam said as he scratched the back of his neck with one hand as he made a call to his men.

Hanging up, he told Ryker, "Grab your hat, were headed over to Pete's house."

"If this was what the Chief's men thought it was, they'd finally found the head of the "Triple Indemnity" ring. However, there was something fishy about this whole thing. Why would Pete Fordson give them permission to toss his home without any fuss, if he knew he had damming evidence in his desk drawer? You just don't forget things like that, particularly if you're capable of masterminding something as intricate as the Triple Indemnity scheme," Sam reasoned.

Within a half hour, Sam and Vincent had arrived and, right behind them, were Shelley and Cal with Ryker and the forensics team. Two other agents were covering the Massey home.

Ryker felt funny entering his boss's home. He knew if Pete found out he'd been there, life as he knew it, would end. He, and the whole staff knew how Pete could be. All but the Abrams brothers hated him and, he wasn't so sure that they didn't also but, they tolerated him out of necessity.

Quickly, the BPD led them to Pete's office and showed them the file. It lay open on top of his desk. After they'd taken a close look at it, they all declared that it was authentic – it was the smoking gun that they'd been looking for all these months. In it were all the names of the people who had been killed, plus many that they'd never heard of, who might be still alive – they'd had to find out - and quick.

Sam asked Jerome and Harold, if they'd touched it and they admitted, rather sheepishly, that they had. Sam and Vincent pulled out several pairs of plastic gloves and all of them put them on, saying, "we would hate to have all this evidence thrown out on a 'contaminated crime scene technicality, wouldn't we," his voice was directed at Harold and Jerome, who were trying to avoid eye contact.

After checking through all the sheets in the folder, then the desk drawers, all the file drawers in the file cabinet and finding nothing, Sam said, "Strange, that this is all there is and to have found it in such an obvious place is almost beyond belief. I cannot believe that such a smart man, one who put together such a brilliant plan would leave evidence in such a stupid place. You'd expect that it would be hidden on a USB drive behind an electrical wall plate or in the dirt in a plant jar or any number of other places - but in the back of a drawer – give me a break!"

They moved on to the master bedroom, with its huge En Suite bathroom and showers, to the sitting room off the bathroom and the two huge walk-in closets. Pete's was organized, with pants running the gambit in colors and shirts and ties the same way. It was an automatic rotating system where with a button he could feed clothes to the dressing area in one continues movement, much like one would see at a dry cleaners. Then they entered Amelia's closet and right away, both Ryker and Shelley spotted something that didn't fit.

Ryker immediately said, "guys, do you see anything wrong here?" Shelley looked at him smiling, as she waited for their answer. They looked closer, but only shrugged – "just looks like a lot of women's clothes to us, they echoed".

"Go ahead, Shelley, tell them what's wrong with this picture."

"To start with, these clothes are all out of style, second, they're not quality or name brands." Then she sniffed them. Wrinkling up her nose, she said, "pee-yoo, I'd say they were fresh from a garage sale, or the Salvation Army racks. From what I've heard about Pete's wife, she went first class – none of this stuff ever touched her skin. I'm betting these have all been changed out and her clothes have been sold – Pete probably had it done, while they were out eating."

Ryker, nodded his head – most of it he could see, but he doubted that Pete would have bothered to sell her clothes – he wasn't the type to take the time. If he'd done it, he would have just had the clothes all picked up and sold wholesale, without replacing them and he wouldn't have done it until long after the heat had died down.

Other than the file folder, which tied Pete to the Triple Indemnity Insurance Fraud case, there was nothing that they could find in the house that would lead them to where Pete's wife was. They signaled the techs to take over, with orders to find any evidence of foul play or anything linking Pete to his missing wife - also to any further evidence linking him to the case. The techs stormed the house, pulling files and computers and taking them back to the lab.

*　　　　*　　　　*

Pete, after being brought in for questioning, accompanied by his lawyer, had been grilled by Detectives Harold Scoville and Jerome Natelli. They were focused on his wife's disappearance and his connection to the "Boomerang Case". They told him that they'd found evidence in his home that tied him to the murders of several people. No matter what he said, they seemed convinced that he was not only involved in his wife's disappearance, but also, in the insurance fraud scheme to defraud the insurance company of millions of dollars by orchestrating the deaths of several people. Finally, upset with their accusations and not being able to reason with them, Pete lawyer demanded that they either charge or release him. As far as Pete was concerned, he might as well have been talking to the wall.

He could only imagine what this farce was doing to his reputation in the field and his office. He'd, no doubt lose his insurance license and his job over this.

"He shouted, "What are you doing about finding my wife"?

His question was answered by a knock on the door - the FBI people had arrived and suddenly things went from bad to worse. Samuel Ohonahee, Regional Director of the FBI and Special Agent, Vincent Rogers of the FBI appeared and sat down opposite Pete and his lawyer.

For a moment, Sam stared at Pete as he gently patted the table with the corner of a file, as if he was contemplating something.

"Maybe you can help us to understand something," he said quizzically. "How is it, that among all your fingerprints, in yours and her car, your home and everywhere she's been, even last night at Station 5, we couldn't raise one single finger print belonging to your wife?"

Pete and his lawyer, sat there dumbfounded.

Then Pete, recovering from this bit of unexpected information, irritably, said, "What ... that's impossible, she lived with me for over five years ... this must be some kind of a mistake," he shouted.

"Not if you went over the house, the cars and at the restaurant, wiped all her prints away, making it look, as if she was never there – who knows, maybe to cover up your crime. We have checked every club and place you said she went and no one ever remembers seeing her - she's like a phantom. All the folks where you work, said they only saw her one time and, even then, you gave her the bum's rush out the door and none of your associates at the conferences you attended, remembers ever seeing her. So, what gives?"

"Nothing gives!" Pete, sneered at Sam and Vincent. "What are you trying to say, that she doesn't exist, that I made her up?"

"No, I'd say she exists, but you had her on a very short leash – maybe even kept her in a special room in your home and only let her out at night for your own deviant sexual pleasures. Why else would you have gone to such lengths to keep her home; building such high walls around your place, an iron gate, cameras everywhere, security up the kazoo?"

"No, you got it all wrong, it was never like that, we both valued our privacy and she could come and go anytime she wanted. We had a loving relationship. She had her hobbies and friends – she was happy, for God sakes. What you're suggesting is just plain ludicrous."

"Okay, you tell us, why there weren't any prints, no pictures of her anywhere in the house, no one we have talked to has ever seen her?"

There was only silence as Pete shrugged his shoulders, "well, she must not have been telling me the truth about where she'd been and what she was doing all this time ... I don't know - I trusted her, what more can I say?"

"Apparently not much," Sam, replied.

Evidently, they were through with him for the time being, as they put him in a holding cell with a couple of kids who were watching something on a phone. He thought absently, that they must have shoved it up their ass to have been able to sneak it past them, since he had been body searched.

"HOLY shit, one of them exclaimed – God, she has a kick like a mule – did you see that ... nearly took that guy's head off."

His interest peaked, he got up, and asked, "May I have a look?"

"Sure, why not, and the guy with the phone played the news segment over again. He could see a large man following a young woman into the parking lot of what looked like a diner. He was hitting on her and she was warning him off. When he reached for her, there was a sudden blur of motion as her foot came up in an arch, striking him in the face. He stumbled backward and fell, she turned and walked out of the camera's range – but something had caught his attention – it was a "tell" and he knew instantly, that his wife was alive. If it hadn't been for the twitch of her shoulder as she turned, he wouldn't have recognized her with the black unkempt hair and the way she was dressed. He had no idea she was trained in the Marshal Arts. More over, he was glad she wasn't dead. He didn't know why she'd left him but, at least, she was free of this mess he found himself in and wouldn't be dragged down with him.

* * *

Back at the insurance office, word had reached them about Pete's situation and the office was divided between Pete being guilty and the other half of the office not believing he was involved. Despite his unpopularity, he had pulled a lot of sympathy votes.

For the time being, Thorn Carbine appointed the senior man on the staff, Ray Thornburg, to take over. By nature, he was a quiet, non-assuming man who vigorously tried to avoid the limelight, at all cost.

With Ray in charge, the staff settled down to a less confrontational dialog during meetings. As a result, the moral got measurably higher and subsequently they all started writing more business. Even though Ryker was busy with the FBI, he still had to find and continue to write business.

*   *   *

Samuel Ohonahee had called a special meeting of all the area agents and the Centerville Police Chief, Bill Myerson. Once seated and the door closed, Samuel cleared his throat, and said, "before this meeting starts, I must stress to you that not a word of what is said in this room goes beyond these walls – does everyone understand?"

"Yes, Sir," the room erupted in unison.

"We are about to exercise a very important warrant – everyone at the disclosed address are to be arrested, the house on the said property, searched and all computers, paper files and phones seized. Once secured, forensics will move in to fingerprint and look for any evidence tying the activities within the house to those who are found there and any other member not there, to the "Boomerang Murders" also known to us as the "Triple Indemnity Case". Also Chief, your men are to be a part of this. Just as we hit the house, you're to cordon off all surrounding streets – no one gets in or out. Also, at the time of the exercise, any hardwired phone services are to be cut. Are there any questions?"

"Okay, let's mount up ... and Chief, you will be deploying your men on a need to know basis – no prior information as to where they're going or why, until they get to the said locations."

In less than thirty minutes, the FBI with over a dozen cars, had moved into position around the house. The phone lines were cut and the men hit both the front and back doors simultaneously. At the same instant, the Police Chief moved his man to all intersections leading into and from the Beethoven property, locking down the whole area.

*　　　　*　　　　*

On the second floor of the Centerville Men's Club, Ben Calvoni was seated at the head of a table made from the finest English Oak, imported from England in the 1800s, along with the chairs. This was a table fit for a king and his court.

I have called this meeting together to report on our "investments" and, to bring up any new business. In front of him lie their ledgers, displaying long columns of figures; money going out and coming in, money in various accounts and where the accounts were located. It also showed their share of the profits right down to their poorest member, who had barely a million dollars to his name.

Just as he was about to hand the envelopes showing what was just deposited into their accounts, to each member, a sound like an explosion, shook the house, echoing all the way up and into their chamber.

Within seconds, men dressed in black, burst into the room with guns in their hands, shouting for them to hit the floor.

Somewhere in the distance, Ben Calvoni heard the words, FBI and he knew his dreams of untold wealth had ended abruptly.

*　　　　*　　　　*

Back in Boston, the hours were ticking by with painful slowness, before word arrived that Lexi was out of surgery, but still in critical condition. She was only allowed one visitor outside of her parent's – her fiancée.

Lexi's parents had arrived during the night from Iowa and were also waiting for any news of their daughter's condition. From time to time, a nurse would come out from surgery and bring them up to date. Twelve hours later, they had finished.

The report was grim. She had sustained a concussion and had not regained consciousness. They had had to bore holes in her skull to relieve the pressure on her brain. Her right arm was broken in two places and had to be pinned. She also had sustained fractures of her right clavicle, six broken ribs, a punctured lung, ruptured spleen, compound fractures of her right leg, broken ankle and multiple injuries to her internal organs. In a word, she was lucky to be alive. When asked how long before she would wake up, the doctor shook his head – we don't know; it may be in a few days, or frankly, she may never gain consciousness. Only time will tell.

During the long hours, both families had come to know each other. Alex had filled them in on the events of the past several days: preparation for graduation, getting a new job, their luncheon and then going on The Spirit of Boston Harbor Cruise where he'd proposed in front of hundreds of people. He had blown her away – it would be a proposal that they'd remember for the rest of their lives. Unfortunately, included in those memories would be the terrible accident that followed. It was not a part that had been planned for their perfect night.

He could still see the night, as he lived it over and over. There had been the high of the day with his proposal to Lexi, then the horrific accident – *"why had it happened to them"*?! He felt like screaming.

Then there was that awful moment – one minute, smiling at each other, holding hands, even though the FBI had just told them of the danger they were in – the extent of which was only just so many meaningless words – until it happened. This had been their day and night and now, someone had stolen their happiness ... *a thief in the night.*

When and if she regained consciousness, the doctors told them it would be a long recovery. They all wept, as they tried to console one another.

Alex would go in for short periods of time and, when he returned, they'd all look at him hoping to see a glimmer of hope – anything that would indicate she was improving.

Finally, the hospital set up cots in the waiting room and a lounge chair for Alex at Lexi's bedside. The night passed and, as the new day dawned, Alex woke to see Lexi's eyes open and staring at him. He could tell by her tears that she was in pain and immediately rang for a nurse.

When she came in, she noted the readings on the instrument's panels and called for a doctor. There was a rush of activity, as they adjusted her meds. After a careful examination, the doctor told him that the pressure had gone down on her brain and that she had normal brain activity. That she was now on that long road to recovery.

Leaning over, he gently kissed her and thanked God for her recovery. As he drew back, she smiled as she held her hand up, to look at her ring – then she smiled again and winked.

Lexi was back and, for better or worse, they had their whole lives ahead of them.

Chapter 12.0

The evidence had been gathered, tagged, cataloged and the files turned over to the Federal and County District Attorney's offices who brought charges against Peter Fordson, which included 20-counts of First Degree Murder and even though her body could not be found, 1-count of second degree murder for one Amelia Fordson, wife of the accused, and also charges for insurance fraud, mail fraud, banking fraud, money laundering and many other lesser charges. Also named in the indictment and charged with 1st degree murder, were Benjamin Calvoni, President of the Centerville Club and all its members, past and present, as well as any and all accomplices, many of which were turning up daily as the search spread from state to state.

All through the months of preparing to go to trial, Jerry Carsdale refused to talk; however, there was enough evidence to charge him with 2nd degree murder, which would, more than likely, get him 30-years to life.

Because Benny Barstow, had turned States Evidence, and had worked with the FBI to bring the syndicate down, he would get perhaps a year and that would be reduced to one year's probation. When the evidence would be presented in court by the District Attorney, concerning the fingerprints in the trucks used to kill Bill Malone and Susan Willis, the defense would prove that the death of Bill Malone was an accident. That one Benny Barstow, had no previous knowledge that he was being used to perpetrate the death of Bill Malone. Further, that Susan Willis had been killed by another hit man and not Benny Barstow, as finger prints in the truck revealed.

The men and women, who had served as Recruiters for the organization, having had no knowledge of the criminal activities that their employers were guilty of, would not be charged. Harold Scoville, also had turned States Evidence and, because of his invaluable help working undercover, would not be charged with any crimes against the government or state but, would be put on departmental probation for 6-months, doing office duties, with the blessings of Internal Affairs.

*   *   *

Several months after the first arrests, the trials were finally getting underway. Federal, State and County trials were to run congruently, so the prisoners and witnesses would have to be shuttled between different courthouses in different cities, causing several delays in other on-going trials.

Every news service and media outlet was devoting most of their resources in covering what was termed the trial of the century. Many believed it to be the biggest story since the 1957 Apalachin Mafia[18], arrests and trials, in Apalachin, NY.

Other than being called to appear as a witness at various trials, Ryker's family life had returned to normal. Life around the insurance office was much

---

[18]   For further information on the Apalachin Mafia meeting, arrests and trials, consult the following website:

http://www.slate.com/blogs/crime/2013/11/14/apalachin_meeting_on_this_day_in_1957_the_fbi_finally_had_to_admit_that.html less stressful, with Pete on a short lease; confined to his home and when he was not at one trial or another. With Pete out of the office, Ray had adapted to his new role as Sales Manager. He was being paid appropriately and seemed happier with his new job and, because of his charming ways, he was always welcome on a sales call.

The switch to selling pension plans, he knew had a nearly 100-percent retention rate and also, being licensed to sell Property and Casualty Insurance, added to his income, not to mention his stipend from the FBI.

*   *   *

During the trial, Pete Fordson had his whole life dragged out for all to see. Pictures were entered into evidence of his wife, Amelia, taken at their very private and rushed wedding. Several pictures that turned up at their home were very private and not meant for the public. When the pictures were first shown, there was an audible gasp from the courtroom. All of them showed a very, vivacious young woman and, when shown next to his picture, the prosecutor raised the specter of her being a trophy wife, young enough to be his daughter. He would go on to tell the jury, that Mr. Peter Fordson, her husband, had also taken out a million dollars of insurance on her, only days after they were married, providing motive - the "why" he'd murdered her.

As Ryker sat in the courtroom, listening to the prosecutor present the state's case, he remembered the glint in Pete's eyes that was as cold as the ice on the Alaskan North slope, when he was made the butt of a joke at the Thatcher's. Then he remembered another time - they had been returning to the office, from their last sales call, when they'd nearly been run over by a truck. Just before it had happened, he had seen two men on the corner and afterwards only one walked away. Pete had refused to admit that he had seen the other man, until he was forced to acknowledge his existence, after seeing him dead at the side of the road. Now he knew why.

Pete didn't want to admit to seeing the man, because it was a hit, one that he had most likely orchestrated. And, what was it with all that security around his home – now, he knew what Pete had been hiding. Then there'd been that bit of information from Ray about Pete having been seen around town recruiting. Presumably, it had been for new insurance agents ... but now, in hindsight, wasn't it probable that he'd been recruiting for his insurance fraud scheme? Pete had recanted that claim, during cross-examination, saying that he'd been recruiting people to work for Joe and himself in a fast food franchise. They had formed a partnership and it would be borne out with Joe Carbine's testimony. Also, he wondered how Pete afforded a mansion, on top of a mountain no less, on the salary of a sales manger? These questions and more kept buzzing around in his mind, begging for an answer.

*   *   *

Even with Pete out of their lives, they still all wondered when he had turned from being a law-abiding citizen, to that of cold-blooded killer. Even so, Ryker would often argue in favor of Pete, pointing out the inconsistencies in what he knew about Pete, as opposed to what the evidence showed. Even the voice recordings, though they sounded like Pete, they still didn't ring true with what he knew of the man. Something just didn't set well with him about Pete's case. Even up to the end of the prosecutor's part of the trial, Pete claimed that he had been framed, but in the end, with his wife's body still missing, he had simply appeared to have given up and accepted what would presumably be a sentence of life without parole. Ryker knew when the trial ended, Pete's house and all his property would go up for auction, as would the properties of all the members of the Centerville Men's Club. All the assets would be attached by the State and Federal Government to cover the costs of the lengthy court trials, as would over a half-billion dollars that had been in offshore accounts, which the State counted on to cover their costs, had suddenly been discovered to have mysteriously disappeared. Even the best manpower that the FBI, CIA and NSA could enlist, couldn't find it.

Finally, after weeks of listening to the Prosecutor present the State's case against Peter Fordson, the State of New York rested their case. Henry Chandler, a young, up and coming lawyer who, it had been whispered in the halls of the State House, had gotten the nod for higher office, and who had just presented the State's case as it's prosecutor was now headed to higher and better things. After listening to his closing, one would have thought he was running for President. It was now time for the Defense to present their case.

*   *   *

It was snowing, dark and cold, when the back, service entrance door to the Station 5 Restaurant, opened and a woman dressed in loose fitting work-clothes with a hairnet over her dark stingy hair, appeared. No doubt, she was one of their many dishwashers. She walked with a limp, carried an old badly scared, faux leather, pocket book with a broken strap and a large plastic bag that read Wegman's on the side. She looked as if she lived on the street, probably in some condemned building on the east side. She scurried out of the overhead lights, to a place in the shadows, where her beat up old car was parked. She opened the creaking door, slid in across the cold vinyl seats and closed the door with a bang, putting her pocket book and bag in the seat next to her. Despite the cold, she sat there for a time watching and listening. It felt good to be in the car, out of the cold and, at this point in her life, a new sense of freedom was slowly setting in.

She started the car, adjusted the heat lever and fan button, and then waited. After about 15 minutes, she heard sirens in the distance. A knowing smile creased her face, as she turned the wipers on to scrape the snow off the windshield. The heat had started to push the coldness out of the car and it felt good. Putting the shift lever into "R", she pushed on the gas peddle and backed the car slowly out of its parking place. As she did, she could hear the crunch of ice and snow beneath the car's cold tires and then she drove past a limo, idling in the shadows cast by the building, and on out of the parking lot. After maneuvering onto the parkway, she drove out Shore Drive until she entered the ramp for 81 and headed south.

It'd been a long day, the last in her life with Peter Fordson. He'd been a good man - for the most part. She knew she wouldn't miss his smoke laden kisses and his indifference to her needs. At first, he'd been able to keep up with her – she was young and she liked sex and she liked it often ... after a few weeks, he slowed down and seemed to become somewhat distant – caught up in his business. He had provided well for her – giving her time to develop her skills and expressed his love for her through giving her expensive gifts.

She remembered the first time they'd met; at first, he'd ignored her and she'd thought she was losing her touch. She had an arrangement with the bar's manager – he knew the score, so long as she bought drinks and kept the customers drinking, he'd look the other way.

She was looking for a ride. It had to be someone who could afford her on a full-time basis. She had an idea; a sort of business plan - but she needed time to develop it and Pete had unknowingly supplied the catalyst. She found him easy to talk with and through their dating, she knew he wasn't an abuser; the kind of man who liked beating women up for their pure pleasure. So, when he suddenly suggested that they get married, she knew that this was her chance, but she had to act as if she wasn't too eager or he might pull back and that would cost her "capital" with him.

When she learned that he was in the insurance business, she knew she'd found the one ingredient that would make her plan work. It was only a matter of learning the ins and outs of it and, over the months that he was at work, she poured over life insurance law and the types of polices that his company sold. He was a very predictable man so she knew when he would be home and timed her departures and arrivals just after and before his, as she didn't want him to think she was staying home all day, or asking questions. So, she'd tell him about this place or that, which she'd been to. The country club and the various charities had been a good cover, as she knew he'd never check them out or be in the least bit interested in going to their functions - that just wasn't him, he'd often tell her. Even so, she made sure to pay their fees with her credit card to cover herself.

His being away every day gave her ample time to study, not only the insurance business, but to get her MBA through SUNY Empire College. This gave her the basis upon which to develop the foundation for her new business model. She knew that, at first, as she got her concept rolling, there would be times in which she'd have to deal directly with the public and this didn't fit into her plans for a "single cell" concept – there had to be no one or anything that would lead back to her. After giving it some thought, she decided to hire an actor – she even wrote a script for him to memorize. She picked an actor from the local theater – they had books filled with the actor's pictures and with the pictures were their names, phone numbers and addresses. She finally found one that suited her purposes; his name was Kevin Sheppard and he bore a strong resemblance to Pete, which was part of her plan. She needed a rabbit for the foxes to chase and he'd due nicely.

She had given Kevin a call, told him about what she wanted and why – she told him that she simply felt it was better for a man to handle certain aspects of hiring people for her company. He'd agreed and she sent him the script of what he was to say and how he was to act. The part demanded that he be forceful and very edgy, and then when he had thought he had perfected the part, he was to send her a tape of his performance. She needed to see if he was convincing or not. After a couple of "takes", she'd approved. These transactions were all handled through a burner phone. After that, it was only a matter of dropping his orders and money at the bus station or at various parks throughout the area. It worked like a charm – she often set off in the distance monitoring his performances, to ensure that there were no slip-ups.

Because of her model-like appearance, she, on varies occasions, had to fight off unwanted advances by wit and stealth. She knew that eventually, she'd run out of luck and would be easy prey for some psycho. So, she decided to do something about it and now was the time. She did some research, found a reportable training center, and took classes, first in Karate where she earned her Black Belt and then she moved on to Kung Fu to broaden her versatility into the circular rhythms of grace and form. She also ventured into Taekwondo, as it offered defense and attack modes involving kicking which was great in building up her sense of balance and legs. These offensive/defensive forms of Marshal Arts, provided her with several things; inner strength, patience, self-control and confidence.

She had been driving for an hour when she saw a truck stop just ahead, and decided to pull off, fuel up and get something to eat.

It was about midnight – perhaps a cup of coffee to go and a couple of donuts would do the trick to keep her awake. She knew from her GPS that a few miles down the road was a Rest Stop where she'd grab a quick nap. Her goal was to drive to Baltimore, ditch her stolen car and fly out to the Caymans, and then on to France, where they didn't allow extradition to the US should someone figure out who she really was, and want to get her back to the states to stand trial.

She'd learned in "past lives", how to forge IDs and hide in plain sight. She was a great fan of the public libraries – their shelves were loaded with "how to books". In her past lives, she'd been dubbed "A Black Widow" for obvious reasons. Now she'd moved on to something much bigger and many times more profitable. She had, yet again, reinvented herself and with it came untold wealth.

She pulled up to the pump, got out, went over to the booth, handed the man a twenty-dollar bill, went back to the car and pumped gas until the machine stopped. Then she drove over to the entrance to the restaurant and parked.

Even at this late hour, the place was humming with long distance drivers. They were fundamentally a rough, tough, rag tag, looking bunch and all smelled of diesel fuel. They were seemingly dividend into two groups; gentle or rowdy. The gentle group was better dressed; usually sporting clean clothes, shaved and much quieter where as, their counterparts were loud, course talking, wore clothes that had not been washed in a week, sported tattoos all over their bodies and had bad breath.

She stepped up to the cashier, ordered her food and paid for it, then retired to one of the few open booths. It was not long before one of the rowdy truckers came over and asked her if she'd like some company. He was a large man with a bloated face, and a voice that sounded like crushed glass. His breath smelled like raw sewage, no doubt from an abundance of visible tooth decay.

The others nearby had quieted their banter as they watched to see if their buddy was going to score. The waitress showed up with her two plain donuts in a small brown paper bag and an insulated coffee container. She was partly successful in chasing the man off, as she made her delivery. Quickly, she got up and was leaving when the man accosted her on the way out the door as his friends cheered him on.

She led him into the parking area and, turning to confront him, she told him that she wasn't interested and to leave her alone. She didn't know whether it was because his friends were all at the windows cheering and jeering, or if he was just full of himself, but he reached for her and, as he did, she let fly her right foot in a roundhouse kick[19] to his head. The impact lifted him off his feet, snapping his head back and to one side. He hit the ground several feet behind where he'd been standing, twitched a couple of times and then laid still. She immediately got into her car, laid her bag down in the seat and put the coffee container in her console, then drove off. She

---

[19] Dollyŏ chagi

was glad to be away from that place and on her way again.

At the rest stop, she pulled in and sought out an area at the far end under some trees where she gulped down the coffee and ate her donuts. It'd been over five hours since she'd last eaten. It hadn't been that much as she'd developed a case of nerves, which caused her to lose her appetite. Feeling nature's call, she was forced to leave the car. She had no way of locking it since she'd used a coat hanger to break into it to begin with, and had hotwired it to get it started. Given how old and badly run down looking it was, she was sure no one would try to steal it.

The woman's restroom was like so many others – smelly, dirty and toilets only half fit to use. Crude things were engraved on the walls in her booth, indicating the availability of various women for sex ... and more. That was a picture she didn't want to allow into her mind.

Reaching for the toilet paper, she discovered that it was nearly out, causing her to have to reach far up into the workings of the device – much further than she would have liked to go. Absently, she wondered how many other women had stuck their nasty hands up there. Finally, she found enough tissue to do the job – she'd report it to the maintenance people on the way out.

While she was in the stall, she pulled out another dress - it was deliberately plain as she didn't want to attract any attention - changed out of her baggy dishwashing jump suit and stuffed it in the plastic bag along with her hair covering, next to the party dress, blond wig and shoes from her last night with Pete. From her pocket book, she took out a comb and brush and fixed her hair, put lipstick on and some eye shadow. Again, the transformation was complete and again, she looked very different from when she'd first entered. Before leaving, she took the large

Wegman's plastic bag and stuffed it far down under all the paper towels in the trash can.

On the way out, she stopped at the map viewing station to see where she was, relevant to where she was headed, and then she headed for the food court with its protracted line of money hungry machines.

Wherever she went, she was careful not to leave any fingerprints. She had learned early in this game, that that was the first "big don't" and the second was like unto it, "don't stick out". She had also learned to avoid security cameras - at all costs. With the new high-tech software, anyone can be tracked aided with the use of powerful facial recognition programs. Seeing camera's mounted at each end of the food court, she decided against getting anything and headed, instead back toward her car.

Some kids she'd just passed were looking intently at their phones, when one of them pointed at her and said – "she looks just like her ... wow, she's the killer."

Her insides froze – better to face them head on than to run away and confirm their intuition.

She walked toward them as she exclaimed, "who looks like me," she asked. All of them looked at their phones and then back at her ... "well, a little bit," one of them said hesitantly.

"Let me see," she said, forcing excitement into her voice, as her hand reached for the nearest phone.

The young girl pushed the play button and she watched as she saw herself take out a truck driver nearly twice her size, then she turned and walked out of the camera's range.

"Wow," she said in mock surprise.

"Holy cow, I wish I could do that shit ... that's totally awesome," she continued, her voice rising in mock excitement.

The kids looked first at her, then at the picture again. "Well, maybe not – you're a lot hotter looking than this lady," another boy said as he looked first at his phone and then at her.

"So, what did the guy do to her that made her go commando on him?" she asked innocently.

"He tried to grab her and she kicked the shit out of him using a Kung Fu kick. She killed him straight out. They say he was dead before he hit the ground, broke his neck clean as a whistle. Boy she's one babe that I wouldn't want to cross, I want to tell you," another one of the boys said, as he shook his head in disbelief.

"Well, if I tried to get my leg that high, I'd fall over and probably break my neck," one of the girls said. They were all nodding; as she knew, they were picturing such an event and not seeing it as a reality, and she agreed with her.

"Any thing more about the story," she probed, just to ensure that she'd successfully thrown them off.

"No, except they're looking for her – probably for Man Slaughter, the guy said.

"Well, let's wish them luck – she's probably a local who just happened to get in a lucky kick," she added to further push them off the track.

"Yeah, I can see that," the young girl replied as they all turned toward a van where their mother was putting a younger child in a booster seat.

"*Wow, that was a close one,*" she breathed – the last thing she needed was someone shooting her picture with a phone and putting it on social media. She'd have to change her looks again, just to get ahead of them. In fact, it was time to change rides. Checking her map, she found a junk yard only a few miles down the road.

After arriving, she was glad that it didn't have a gate or any cameras that she could see, and no one was around. Quickly she drove in, parked the car behind a pile of rubble, got out, tore the license plate off and used it to deface the inspection sticker. Then she threw it as hard as she could into a distant pile of steel. Now the car would be virtually impossible to track back to its owner. Usually, in places like this, they didn't have time, or the means to track Vin numbers. It would more than likely be crushed in a few days and that would be the end of it.

She quickly walked out of the lot and down the road to a mom and pop diner where she ordered coffee and then went to the Lady's room. She'd checked before entering and, like the junk yard, they also had no camera's, not even near the register. *"Trusting bunch,"* she thought – *"innocence is a wonderful thing if you live in the sticks"*. But, out there in the real world, the vultures would be picking your eyes out of your head if you didn't protect everything you had.

When she came out, she'd razored her black hair shorter – like a fluffy Pixie cut and, again, she'd poked all the hair scraps down under the paper towels. Slowly, she was remaking herself into someone else. With the updated look, she'd have to change her ID. To do that, she'd have to go to a mall where the chances were greater to find someone that looked like her.

Since it was lunchtime, she ordered a tossed salad with Balsamic Vinaigrette dressing and ice water. The atmosphere spoke to the age of the place. It looked more like someone's home than a diner. The woman running it looked to be old enough to be someone's grandmother. She could hear her humming as she worked on her salad. The area had only a small bar that was used for serving and a handful of tables, with no two alike. There were no table menus, the selections were posted on the wall over the counter and appeared to have been the same over as many years as the diner had existed.

In no time, she was served her salad, along with a freshly folded napkin and her cold drink of water. "Is there anything else I can do for you sweetie," she chirped.

She shook her head, "no", as she smiled back at the woman.

As she watched out of the window, she'd see a car or truck go by every so often and marveled at how little traffic this area had. Truly, they were off the main routes of travel. She made a mental note of this for future use.

After finishing her salad, she got some money out of her pocket book and laid it on the table, asking the woman, "If there was any type of transportation from here to the nearest mall".

She looked thoughtful for a moment, and then replied, "Well there's a bus that comes through here about every hour and Lennie could stop by if you want, he's our cab driver. He could take you in if you didn't want to wait for the bus. I'd be happy to call him, if you want," she added with a certain amount of excitement in her voice. Apparently, there was something going on between the two of them and, judging by the twinkle in her eyes, it wasn't Pinnacle.

"Okay, call Lennie; I trust he'd be faster than waiting for the bus?"

"Oh, my goodness, yes and he knows where everything is, so you wouldn't have to worry about getting lost."

In no time, Lennie arrived with a cab that belonged in the Smithsonian. She got in and, true to the old women's word, he got her there in under 15-minutes.

She asked what she owed and he said, five dollars and she gave him a ten and told him to keep the change. He was as pleased as if she'd given him a hundred dollars.

Once in the mall, it was decidedly cooler and very modern. Again, she kept her eyes open for cameras as she scanned the women in the stores who were walking by. Finally, after several hours, she spotted a look alike. She was shopping in a Saks off 5th store. So she started working her way closer, to the point where she knew that their paths would cross. She waited until the woman had put her pocket book down and was checking out a garment on the rack, Amelia had grabbed an arm full of dresses and, as she swooped by, she picked up the women's pocket book and headed for the changing room. Only the most skilled eye would have caught the snatch.

Once in the change room, she emptied the woman's purse into hers and then discarded the stolen purse in a trashcan on the way out. Next, she purchased some new clothes, a pocket book and some luggage, using the woman's charge cards. After changing her clothes, she left the mall, picked up a commuter bus that took her on into Allentown; from there she'd grabbed a bus to the Lehigh Valley International Airport and a flight out to Atlanta where she made a connection with a flight to the Cayman's. She'd used her own cash to buy her tickets; she didn't want to risk anyone tracking her through the stolen credit cards.

*   *   *

Benjamin Desoto, a man of advanced years, was no new comer to the court room – no, he'd served over 45-years defending some of the toughest, no win cases that could or would ever be brought against a man, woman or child and had won all of them. He was tough as nails and knew the law like his own name, and he didn't come cheap.

Pete, after hearing his lawyer, Bill Harrison, a man he'd known most of his life, tell him that given the massive evidence against him that he recommended that Pete throw himself on the mercy of the court. Frankly, he didn't see how he could defend Pete against such overwhelming and convincing evidence.

Pete knew it looked bad, but there had to be some evidence ... somewhere, that was in his favor and it was more than evident that Bill really didn't think he had a chance in hell of winning, innocent or not. He'd given it a lot of thought and decided if he was going down, it wouldn't be without one hell of a fight and to do that, he needed the best that money could buy.

"Bill, if it were you standing in my shoes right now, who would you hire to defend yourself ... knowing that you're innocent of all this?" as he said it, he made an encompassing gestured with his hand.

"Well, if cost was of no consequence, I'd reach out and hire Benjamin Desoto – never knew him to lose a case. Frankly, he's been known to pull more than one rabbit out of a hat, even if he had to hire someone to shoot it ... if you get my drift.

"Then make it happen – I need a hired gun, at this point someone who isn't afraid to kick the shit out of the Prosecutor's ass.

From the time that Benjamin Desoto signed on, it was a day and night blizzard of activity. He was issuing orders even before he left his home in California and again non-stop while on his private plane to Centerville. Within 24-hours of arriving, the defense team was set up and operating. To save time, offices were rented just down the street from the courthouse where the case was to be tried. Anything and everything related to the case or even remotely associated with it had to be obtained, scanned and cataloged online. That meant putting together a massive database.

The first thing he did was to get Pete released; he needed easy and immediate access to the defendant. He found a moderate judge, got bail set and paid the bond, then hauled Pete into his office for a face-to-face meeting.

Once more, Pete told his story. Afterwards, Ben dug in to his story, to mine even the most minute details – things that Pete had to dig deep into his memory to find. Like, Ben often would say, "We got to work to get at the cream and then it has to be churned to make butter".

Before he was done, he gathered more information, like the drawings of Pete's home and a layout of the grounds, and then a list of every person Pete had ever talked to or done business with over the past five years. He acquired copies of all Pete's bank and savings accounts, lists of purchases and where he'd made them, also lists of relatives and business associates. When he was done, Pete was not only exhausted, but Ben knew more about him than Pete knew about himself.

I see where the prosecution has questioned your life style; big house on the hill, on an insurance man's salary; not realizing that you inherited a small fortune from your grandfather's estate. So ... that will be easy to knock down.

"It's obvious that you treated your wife very well. I see here that you bought her a very nice new car awhile back – do you still have it?"

"Why, yes ... did you know that it has a GPS?"

"No, I didn't," Pete answered, somewhat perplexed about where Ben was going with this.

"I also noticed that you have a "secret, harden, safe room" in your home ... Ben paused, and then continued, "When was the last time you've been in it?"

"Oh, I'd say, a couple of years."

"Do you know if your wife's been in it?"

"No, I can't say ... not to my knowledge, though after we were married, I did tell her about its existence, why I had it and how to access it."

"Has anyone from law enforcement entered it?"

"No, not that I know of – in fact unless they had the house drawings, they wouldn't have known it exists and they haven't asked me, either."

Over the next day, Ben continued obtaining bits and pieces of information, from the GPS. From it, they learned every place Pete's wife had frequented, since getting the car. When they discovered that the house had a safe room, Ben decided to check it out – wouldn't do any harm and he wanted a look at it to see if one of these might fit his needs in his home. So, he took some time out, from working on the case, and personally accompanied his forensics team as they entered the "safe room". Since the house was still under quarantine, as part of the crime scene, the FBI had to be notified and be at the scene during the investigation. Sam decided to take the trip over and called on Ryker to accompany them.

Using the drawings, they pulled the designated book in the bookcase, which resulted in the click of a latch within the wall and a section of bookcase swiveling toward them a few inches. Taking a hold of the frame, Ben pulled and the door opened fully revealing an opening through which they could pass into another large room.

They all could tell immediately, that it had recently been in use, as all the furniture had been displaced and piled along the wall, leaving the center of the room vacant.

Ben started walking in circles, rubbing his heavily whiskered chin and squinting his eyes, as he appeared to be thinking.

Sam saw the way the room was arranged and could visualize how it had been decorated and reasoned that someone had used this space – but for what? As he pondered the "what", he noticed Ryker circling the room, looking at the floor.

"What are you seeing, Ryker?" Sam asked, barely audible, as he walked past Ryker with his head down and turned away from the others.

"Tell you later," was all he murmured.

Ryker had slowly surveyed the space and noted several deep symmetrical impressions in the carpeting, impressions that were slowly being filled in as the fibers in the carpet sprang back, reclaiming their original shape and space. The space, between the impressions, had the appearance of having had a couple of tables and a chair set up in the area. So, a set of tables had been set up – *"why? he'd ask himself. Perhaps to do some work where you didn't want to be interrupted or seen," he reasoned. Now if he didn't want to be seen or interrupted, he might be doing something that he didn't want anyone to know about – and where would he stash his stuff where he could get at it from time to time, and where it would be out of sight? Aaaah, a storage area ... and most even had pickup and delivery service. A lot of people these days, he knew were moving in or out of an area and needed a temporarily place to store their personal things without fear of having them stolen. So, a whole industry had sprung up to fill this need.*

Now to find out if and where Mrs. Fordson had stored her things, since Pete had denied having been in the space for two or more years.

Once outside and in the car, Ryker told Sam about his suspicions.

"Okay, sounds good." Sam said, "That's why we pay you the big bucks." He said with a smile, as he immediately launched into having his people locate and flash Amelia's picture around all the storage places in the Triple Cities. It wasn't long before they got a hit at a storage place out towards Apalachin. They were ordered to stand in place, until Sam and a forensics team could get out there.

Ryker could feel the excitement in their voices ... something big was about to happen, he could feel it in the air – finally, they were about to see something tangible in regards to Pete's wife.

The lock was cut, the door pushed up and all their mouths dropped open.

It was like walking into a treasure trove of evidence. To their surprise, they discovered clothes, cosmetics – just about every personal item Amelia owned. They soon discover that her fingerprints were present on all of it and her DNA. So now they had proof positive, that Pete's wife had moved all this stuff here, by herself, probably intending to come back at some later date to retrieve it or have someone else get it, since she knew Pete would be in prison.

Ryker said, "no, I'm sure she was going to let the rent run out and the stuff auctioned off for the rent due on the unit. In this way, her past would be gone forever. She really hadn't counted on us guessing that she had moved all this to a rental unit, so had not taken any further precautions".

Somewhere in every carpet, there's a needle - you just have to search a little harder to find it.

*   *   *

A few hours later, Sam asked Pete, "Did you know that your wife has a rather lengthy record, and that her real name is Viola Weatherly?"

Pete shook his head, "no", with a look of surprise on his face.

"Did you know that during the time you were married, she graduated SUNY with a MBA[20], and acquired a Black Belt in both Karate and Taekwondo?

Again, Pete shook his head, "no".

"We also discovered another passion of your wife's – electronics. She'd bought and learned how to use some very sophisticated equipment and software to

---

[20] Masters in Business

change voice waveforms. In other words, we can prove that she made recordings of your voice and patched together your words into phrases, to be used in her new business venture, one that she designed. From this technology, she graduated to using a voice transformer[21] to turn her voice into yours on a phone. Moreover, if that wasn't enough, she read a ton of books on insurance law and your product lines, particularly those areas describing the legalities of 'Triple Indemnity", which were also highlighted. Now for the real gem in all of this, we found her plan, the one she used to form a "single cell", highly portable, scalable business that she put into place, and when Bata tested in this area, and found to be highly successful, she had it exported to several other states. This plan resulted in both "The Boomerang File" of the BPD and the FBI's "Triple Indemnity Murder File" which had been merged into just the "Triple Indemnity Insurance Fraud Case" - FBI File(s) 36-02356 with several sub-folders. So, Pete, there is no doubt, that we now have the evidence to exonerate you and to get you permanently released, or we will make a mockery out of the DA's case and him in a very public way. I have a feeling that he will want to save his honor and will move to dismiss all charges against you."

Within an hour after setting up a meeting with the Judge and the DA, and reviewing all the new evidence, both the DA and the Judge agreed that there was sufficient evidence to prove Pete Fordson's innocence, and the judge moved to cancel Pete's trial and moved to have Pete freed. However, such evidence just discovered would be made available to all other District Attorneys, immediately.

Later, the Judge signed multiple warrants for the arrest of Viola Weatherly on multiple counts of murder, mail fraud and the list went on for several

---

[21] Voice modulator to change voices

pages. Wanted posters and copies of Warrants were wired to all police, FBI and other judicial offices across the US and its Territories. In addition, the warrant went out to all overseas law enforcement offices in other countries, which also include Interpol.

The files would remain open, so long as Viola Weatherly remained at large and with a reward set at $100,000.00, for information leading to her arrest; it would be only a matter of time before someone would be in touch with them. In the meantime, her picture would be in the facial recognition database and would be continually scanned against the billions of images that came through the system worldwide in real time. They knew that at some point, she'd slip up, they always did and her imagine would be matched with the one in the database and a signal would be sent to the nearest FBI headquarters as to her location and arrest warrant.

*   *   *

A special meeting was called by the FBI Regional Director of the Centerville Office, Samuel Ohonahee. Ryker had been the last to arrive with Cal, who was under orders not to bring Ryker in until Samuel called. Ryker had been led to believe that it was just a general meeting to tie up all the lose ends from the case. But, when he arrived and entered the conference room, he saw some of his insurance friends and all the local agents and some from the other offices – even the manager from the Stratford office was there. Then he spotted his wife, Katie with Shelley and knew that something was up – as she never had attended one of their meetings. Their arrival was cheered by all that were in attendance and Samuel immediately signaled for him to join him on their makeshift stage.

He felt a little shaky as he was not use to this much attention and usually shunned it, if at all possible. Sam seeing his reluctance, grabbed a hold of Ryker's hand drew him up behind the podium along side of him, shaking his hand as he did.

Ryker hardly heard a word he said as he went on about how he had been instrumental in breaking this case. For his efforts, he was given a citation by the FBI Head office for his exemplary work and offered a full-time job as an FBI Consultant. Looking at Katie, seeing her smiling and nodding, he accepted the offer.

They both felt it was safer than being an insurance man.

*   *   *

By nightfall in the BVI, she'd arrived and after picking up her luggage, she'd hailed a cab and headed for the Ritz-Carlton Grand Cayman. The door attendant took her luggage and once she'd checked in, she headed to her room – she couldn't wait to get a bath and change into some clean clothes. After the door attendant had deposited her things in her room, she tipped him and locked the door.

Finally, she'd arrived. Now to get her ID's updated, to her new name, her clothes cleaned and that long awaited bath. Tomorrow she was going to be personally checking in at her banks to update the information on her accounts.

She'd also be buying a computer, and once she'd gotten it; she'd make a few tweaks, making it invisible, something else she'd learned. With this one, she could continue to move money around and track her balances. She knew that for some time, her accounts would continue to grow by virtue of all the policies that were "maturing" and those yet to be written.

At last check, and after adding all the accounts together, she'd collectively passed the half billion-dollar amount and before long, she'd be a billionaire. Gone were the days of being dirt poor - working bars and sleeping with men to make ends meet. Now, she could be selective with whom she spent her time and how.

The following day, she made the rounds of her banks, updating account information, opening and transferring money to the new accounts, thereby leaving the original accounts zeroed out. With auto-transfer orders in place to redirect any money slated to be deposited in the old account, immediately transferred it to the new accounts, thereby never showing any money in the original account, but still acting as a conduit. It was a clever plan, to anyone who did not understood the workings of this type of account, it would appear that the account was a derelict account and subsequently not being used any longer.

Outside of the hotel, a phone call was being made. It was the door attendant, "another one has landed," he said in a low voice, as if someone might over hear him. On the other end of the line, another voice said, *"Let the games begin"*.

"The best laid plans of mice and men often go awry." The saying adapted from a line in "To a Mouse," by Robert Burns

END

ABOUT THE AUTHOR

Philip R Morehouse (P. R. Morehouse) was born in upstate New York. Among his many jobs, he worked as a writer for over 50-years and he was also a professional photographer. Now retired, he pursues his interest in writing true-to-life, survival, and adventure-type stories.

Other books written by the author are:

- *The Wanderer*
- *The Recluse*
- *Retribution*
- *Flash Back*
- *The Benton Harbor File*
- *The Man Without a Country*
- *Ten Dollars a Week – Room and Board*
- *Three Squares and a Rack (US NAVY)*

89430494R00126

Made in the USA
Columbia, SC
21 February 2018